IN THE SKY

DAVID JOWSEY

Kedzie Press International
37 Rosebank Grove
London E17 6RD England

Suite 8042
2647 N. Western Avenue
Chicago, Illinois 60647 USA

Visit us on the World Wide Web at:
www.kedziepress.com

First published 2007

Published by Kedzie Press under license from Sigel Press.

Cover art and illustrations by David Jowsey
Cover design and Interior design by Harp Mando

ISBN: 1-934087-43-2 and 978-1-934087-43-5

A catalogue record for this book is available from the Library of
Congress.

Typeset in: 10pt Columbus MT

In North America: Printed and bound in the United States
In Europe: Printed and bound in the UK by Henry Ling Limited,
Dorchester.

The publisher's policy is to use paper manufactured from sustainable
forests.

The author will make a donation from the proceeds of every copy sold
to his local Children's Hospice, Zoe's Place.

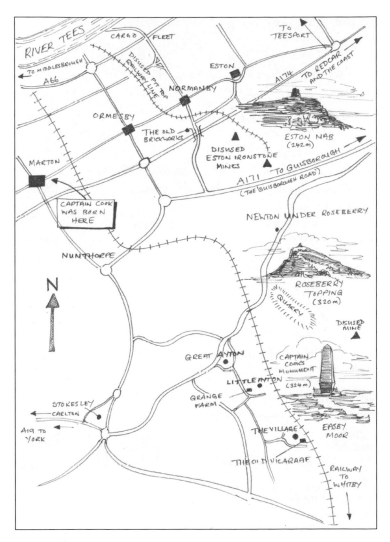

RIVER TEES

CARGO FLEET

TO TEESPORT

TO MIDDLESBROUGH
A66

DISUSED PIT TOP RAILWAY LINE

ESTON

A174

TO REDCAR AND THE COAST

NORMANBY

ORMESBY

THE OLD BRICKWORKS

ESTON NAB
(242 m)

DISUSED ESTON IRONSTONE MINES

MARTON

A171 TO GUISBOROUGH
(THE GUISBOROUGH ROAD)

CAPTAIN COOK WAS BORN HERE

NEWTON UNDER ROSEBERRY

NUNTHORPE

N

ROSEBERRY TOPPING
(320 m)

QUARRY

DISUSED MINE

GREAT AYTON

LITTLE AYTON

CAPTAIN COOKS MONUMENT
(324 m)

GRANGE FARM

STOKESLEY
CARLTON

A19 TO YORK

THE VILLAGE

EASBY MOOR

THE OLD VICARAGE

RAILWAY TO WHITBY

0045053111

ACKNOWLEDGEMENTS

In writing *Dragons in the Sky*, I turned to the following sources to provide me with historical facts:

Cleveland Ironstone Heritage
Produced by Scarborough Borough Council Community Programme Agency

Eston and Normanby Ironstone Mines
Richard Pepper
Published by South Bank and Eston Intimes Past
1987

Ironstone Mining in Eston
A Personal account
W E Brighton
Cleveland Ironstone Series
Industrial Archaeology of Cleveland
Published by Peter Tufts
1996

North York Moors O/S Tourist Map 2
Published by Ordinance Survey, Southampton.
1984

Open Skies Close Minds
Nick Pope
Published by Simon and Schuster Ltd.
1996

I also wish to thank:

The Ministry of Defence, Whitehall, London; RAF Boulmer and RAF High Wycombe for information regarding operational procedures.

In addition, I would like to thank my family and friends for their unwavering support, my colleagues at Ravensworth Junior School for their invaluable advice and encouragement, and for class testing the novel, Andy Taylor for the inspiration, Sue Urwin for her enthusiasm and insight, and everyone who has taken the time to read and comment on my work.

Finally, and without whose expert help and guidance this book would have never been published, I would like to thank my publisher, Thomas Sigel, Josh and Jessica McLarey at Kedzie Press International, my editor Andrew Hogbin and my typesetter Harp Mando. Thank you all.

Visit my website at: www.davidjowsey.com and www.dragonsinthesky.com

ABOUT THE AUTHOR

David Jowsey was born and raised in Middlesbrough, and continues to live and work in the area. He trained as a primary school teacher at Bretton Hall College, Wakefield, where he studied Visual Arts, graduating in 1988. He started his teaching career at Tedder Junior School and is currently a teacher at Ravensworth Junior School in Normanby.

In his spare time David enjoys art and music. He was a founder member of the Band of '78 where he became a competent trombone player, and now shares his skills and experience teaching local children within the band.

David's knowledge of the local area, along with his art skills, have enabled him to illustrate his first novel.

AUTHOR'S NOTE

The events depicted in this book are based around supposed real-life UFO encounters. None are more talked about, even after more than half a century, than the crash at Roswell, New Mexico, in 1947.

There has long been a mystery surrounding Roswell. Some say it happened, some say the Government of the United States covered something up and is still covering it up today. I'll leave that up to the reader to decide.

Rendlesham Forest and the Belgian UFO sightings are documented sightings. Open any book on the UFO phenomenon or enter any related website and you are sure to find reference to them, as well as many other reported encounters.

So if my book has piqued your interest, please delve deeper.

The Village doesn't exist. It is a figment of my imagination but its location is real. All other locations do exist, including Great Ayton. It has all the relaxed qualities I have depicted in this book but I've taken liberties with the arrangement of a few buildings and the interior of the library. I hope any residents of Great Ayton won't take offence at my shifting things around and understand that I only did it because it fitted with the needs of my story.

This is my first book and I hope you have enjoyed reading it as much as I have enjoyed writing it.

David Jowsey
December 2006

For my daughter Ellie-May,
because every moment
I spend with you
is priceless.

CHAPTER 1

Unbeknown to Tom Richards, events that summer were about to change the course of his life dramatically.

Had he foreseen what was about to befall him, it was doubtful he would have been able to do anything about it anyway. But perhaps it was best he didn't see the very thing which was going to knock him flat on his back; the very thing which would leave him feeling as though his world had been turned upside down.

In Tom's case, it really was better not to know.

As soon as he opened his eyes, Tom Richards groaned. He felt the warm heaviness of the air and could almost smell the heat which baked the countryside, locking it in a vice-like grip. Even at such an early hour the heat lingered from the night before. The air felt sticky and he knew it was going to be another unpleasant day.

Tom spent the early part of the morning mooching about in his room, fiddling with this, tinkering with that, but as the day stretched towards noon a dusty heat-haze formed across the distant hills. The horizon shimmered and distorted and the landscape melted and reformed the way faces quickly grow and change in the flames of an open fire. Only the trees offered any welcome shade, their leafy branches casting dappled glimmers of sunlight across the cool grass beneath.

Thrusting his hands into his pockets, Tom stepped outside into the oppressive heat. Sighing, he shuffled his feet grumpily before kicking out at a stone. He watched as it skittered its way across the lawn, disappearing from sight in a clump of long grass. With a mutter he toed at the hard ground before him, digging up clumps of dry earth with a scuffed training shoe before finally losing interest and sloping off towards the corner of the house.

Stepping into shadow, Tom looked up at his home. Admittedly, the Old Vicarage was an impressive building, but it wasn't the house that appealed to him. It was the surroundings.

Tom cast his eye over the skyline. He had learned some of the local landmarks during the last year but his Dad knew them all from his childhood. He was eager to show his family where he had grown up, and when work had offered him the opportunity to leave Manchester and return home he'd jumped at the chance, and mum had been more than happy to give up her florist's job. Now she indulged her creative side as painter. She'd even sold a couple but hadn't made much from them. 'Painting is a route to poverty,' she often said. 'You'll be living on the bread-line if it's left to me.'

Tom's younger sister, Abi, thought their new home was fabulous, but then she was eight, two years younger than Tom and happy in the world of her imagination. She would play amongst the trees, make fairy houses between the roots and sit in the shade to read, whereas Tom wanted to be off doing other things. Sometimes they would have a game of hide and seek using the apple trees, shed and dry stone walls as hiding places, but, after a while, even that lost its appeal.

Tom felt as though he should be allowed more freedom to go wherever he wanted – there were so many things he wanted to do, so many places he wanted to explore, but he was tied by his parents' reluctance to let him roam free. He had a sense of anticipation, a sense of something waiting out there for him and he was desperate to find it.

With a sigh of frustration he crossed the lawn and sauntered towards the gate where he leant against the stone pillar, its stonework warm in the heat of the sun. A lone dog trotted past, glancing casually in Tom's direction, but it neither slowed nor paid him any real attention: Tom was as interesting to the dog as it was to him.

Leaning his chin on his arms Tom drifted, but a sound broke into his thoughts and he looked up into the sky trying to trace its source. He squinted into the bright sunlight as two fighters closed the distance from the horizon. The sky was suddenly filled with the hard edged throaty roar of their engines as the planes raced towards him. Within seconds they were overhead, seeming to skim the rooftops before leaving the village behind, dwindling to dark specks as they disappeared towards the north. Tom watched until there was nothing left to see and their sound faded. Silence returned.

He was just about to turn and walk away when another sound split the air. It was a highly charged crackling sound, as if something electrical was sparking and burning out. The air seemed to vibrate with it. He could feel it in his chest the way the concussion of a powerful firework can sometimes be felt on Bonfire Night, the sound all around, yet not seeming to originate from anywhere in particular. Then, as suddenly as it had begun, it ceased.

'That's funny,' murmured Tom. He quickly looked around, hoping to catch a glimpse of something, anything which might explain the sound he had just heard.

He stood and listened for a little while longer, but, just as he began to lose interest, the air was assaulted by one final crack like a tree snapping under immense pressure, followed by a rolling echo from the direction of the hilltops.

Then all was still.

CHAPTER 2

Tuesday dawned, grey and miserable. Cloud stretched like a blanket over the village and looked a permanent feature of the day, but by mid-morning the heavy clouds had begun to dissipate and blue sky was at last peeping through, the sun finally making its entrance just before eleven o'clock. As lunch time approached, only a few thinning cumulus clouds could be seen to prove that the day had been any different, and the heat soon returned with a vengeance.

Tom spent the morning in the corner of the dining room playing games on the PC while Abi sat reading. Neither had much to do with each other until lunchtime, when, over ham sandwiches and a drink of fresh orange, Mum asked them what they intended to do for the rest of the day.

'I'd like to go to the library,' said Abi. 'I've read the books I borrowed last time and want to look for something different.'

'That's a good idea,' said Mum. 'Why don't you look for that book your teacher told you about? *True Life Adventures*, wasn't it? I bet that'll be really exciting.'

'I think I might,' said Abi, thoughtfully munching her way through a biscuit.

'And what about you?' inquired Mum as she looked at Tom. 'I wish you would read a bit more. There must be lots of books that you'd enjoy.'

Tom groaned inwardly. He wasn't over-enthusiastic

about the library. To him it smelled of old paper and dust and was far too serious. Everyone had to whisper and, if you made too much noise, the librarian *shushed* you from his place behind the counter. He was a bit scary too. Tom found going to the library was never an enjoyable experience, but, after thinking it over, he reluctantly agreed. 'I suppose there might be something,' he muttered. 'Dunno what, though.'

'Well unless you look you won't know, will you, darling?'

Tom sat back and sighed, twisting his mouth while he thought. 'What about what I want to do?'

'Well what do you fancy?' asked Mum.

Tom half smiled. 'Can we go up into the woods? You're always saying we should spend more time out in the fresh air…?' He left the question hanging, knowing full well that he had his Mum right where he wanted her.

She smiled and started to laugh. 'You planned that and I walked right into it. You little monkey!' They all laughed and Mum smiled her *okay, you win* smile, her eyes twinkling. 'Eat up and we'll get off then,' she said. 'I've got a few errands to run myself, but when we get back, I'll sit in the woods with my sketch book while you both run around and no doubt manage to get yourselves filthy.'

Mum didn't really mind. She always said that *children should be allowed to play, and play often involves muck. It's healthy. How can you play while you're constantly thinking about keeping clean?*

Gran never agreed and made *tutting* sounds whenever Tom and Abi came in dirty, but they both thought Mum encouraged it more whenever Gran visited. Dad always said she had a wicked streak. He enjoyed sitting back and watching the whole drama unfold as Gran bristled with the effort of keeping her tongue between her teeth, which she rarely could.

'Right, let's get cleared up then,' said Mum as she pushed her chair away from the table and began collecting the lunchtime pots. Tom sat for a few seconds then passed over his plate.

After helping to clear away, Abi went upstairs to fetch her library books, but Tom stood looking out of the kitchen window at the hills. He must have been staring for quite a while because Mum gently rested her hands on his shoulders and asked what he was thinking about.

'Oh, I was just wondering what that funny noise was yesterday,'

'What noise?' asked Mum. 'I didn't hear anything.'

Tom turned. 'It was like… well, I can't really describe it… like something…something weird was happening, y'know?'

Mum looked puzzled. 'Sorry, but I didn't hear anything. Anyway, I'm sure it was nothing to worry about. Now…' she looked at him intently for a few seconds, her brow furrowed, '…you run upstairs and brush your teeth. You've got a piece of bread stuck between them.'

Tom started to pick at his teeth with his finger but Mum slapped it away playfully. 'Use your toothbrush, not your finger, you mucky article!'

Tom grinned and headed for the stairs. He couldn't help thinking that yesterday's sound was more than just nothing. It was so out of the ordinary. It was so strange. *So weird.*

He paused at the landing window and looked out again. He'd never heard anything like it before.

CHAPTER 3

Abi sat on the floor of the library, a pile of books scattered around her legs, while Mum sat on a chair beside her. They talked in giggling whispers about the book between them, turning the pages with excitement before moving onto another.

On the opposite side of the room Tom, clearly uninterested, wandered between the wooden bookshelves and pulled occasional titles from the shelves, more by chance than the promise of their spines. He lifted a small book about steam locomotives from a shelf at head height and glanced briefly at it before turning up his nose and reaching to put it back.

Thunk! Click!

Tom jumped.

He looked towards the sound and realised it was the librarian, Mr. Lampard, stamping the books of a younger boy Tom thought he recognised. The boy turned slightly and Tom saw it was William Blakely. He didn't know him too well and hadn't had much to do with him all last year.

Thunk! Click!

Mr. Lampard made his final stamp and William smiled politely as the books were closed. Catching the smile, Mr. Lampard furrowed his eyebrows and gave a short, unfriendly grunt before pushing the books across the counter. William scurried from the desk towards the open door and the friendliness of the summer day beyond while Mr. Lampard made adjustments to his desk. Satisfied all was in order, he turned towards Tom. It was then that their eyes locked.

Tom saw the whole movement – the turn of the head, the waving of the curly white hair like that of a diver under the ocean, and the icy stare – in slow motion. He froze. A warm rush of adrenaline pulsed through his body followed immediately by a cold jolt of fear. He turned back to the shelf, his left hand still holding the book half on and half off the shelf.

Bid – a – boom! Bid – a – boom!

Tom's heart was beating like a sledge hammer and his legs were trembling. *Why do I feel so frightened?* The thought flashed through his mind like a lightening bolt and he tried to calm himself, but could still feel Mr. Lampard's eyes burning into his skull across the empty floor of the library.

With an effort of will, Tom turned his head towards the librarian's desk, but Mr. Lampard was gone.

With his chest aching and fit to burst, Tom realised he had been holding his breath. He exhaled loudly. Sucking in fresh air, he tasted dust, the stale aroma of old paper and the waxy smell of polish. Returning the book to the shelf, he stepped forward on trembling legs and turned the corner to see Abi and his Mum heading towards him.

Mum smiled, a sight Tom was only too happy to see. 'Find anything?' she whispered.

Tom opened his mouth to speak but nothing emerged. He swallowed hard and decided to shake his head instead. That way his voice wouldn't betray how scared he had just been feeling.

'Come on then, let's go.' She headed for the desk, Abi close behind her.

Tom hung back, not wanting to approach the desk just yet. He didn't want to come face to face with Mr. Lampard until he really had to. He peered from the seclusion of the shelves as Abi stepped up to the check out and was surprised to see Mr. Lampard smile and speak quietly to her. *Oh well*, Tom thought, *maybe he's not that bad after all.*

Tom was about to step forward when he felt a cold chill run down his spine. As he shivered, the world around him slowed and stopped.

He was aware of a fly which had been buzzing around all afternoon, now momentarily caught in mid flight, its wings unmoving while dust hung suspended in the beams of bright sunlight which slanted in through the high windows. Tom turned, his attention drawn to his hand as it gripped the shelf. His skin seemed to shimmer slightly and he turned his hand over before his face, inspecting it. Lifting his other hand, he saw it too was glowing. He was aware of every line, every crease, every mark. His hands shone brilliantly.

Tom looked around, opening his mouth to speak but couldn't make a sound. While the world around him sat motionless, frozen in time, movement and light by the desk caught his eye, the same desk where his Mum and younger sister now stood, bathed in a purple-white light which crackled and sparked with silent energy.

Abi and Mr. Lampard stood linked by arcs of bright shimmering light. Except it wasn't Mr. Lampard. Tom's mouth and throat instantly went dry as he watched the intense light connecting them, its luminescence bathing them in a shimmering haze. Within it, writhing tendrils enveloped Abi before settling around her head.

Tom tried to move, tried to step forward to help his sister, but his movements were thick as though swimming through treacle. And while Tom stood, unable to move, the tall figure turned its head slowly towards him, its dark eyes searching, boring into him.

The dream-like figure raised its hand. Slender fingers seemed to reach out towards Tom while a voice filled his head. It seemed to echo around as if looking for a place to settle and Tom took a few seconds to realise it was speaking in English. His consciousness finally accepted the voice and the words registered.

You will understand.

In a flash the world was as it had been: Mum and Abi were chatting pleasantly at the desk with Mr. Lampard while the lone Bluebottle buzzed its crazy course high above the room. The familiar *Thunk! Click!* of the library stamp broke into Tom's fuddled brain and he shook his head. Then, without warning, he slumped against the bookshelves and knew no more.

* * *

Afterwards, as he sat on the library steps in the fresh air,

Tom soon came round. 'Are you alright? What happened?' Mum's voice was tight with concern.

Tom looked up, a puzzled expression on his face. 'I don't know. I remember watching you both with the librarian and then everything went fuzzy. I think I just fainted.' He smiled a weak, apologetic smile at his sister who sat with her arm around his shoulders.

'You frightened me,' Abi said, tears threatening to overspill and run down her flushed cheeks, but somehow she managed to check them.

'Sorry.' He gave her a small hug and tried to stand up but a firm hand gently pushed him back.

Tom looked around to see Mr. Lampard smiling down at him. 'You alright, Sonny?'

Tom recoiled. Startled, the figure lifted his hand quickly away. 'Sorry. Didn't mean to make you jump.'

'I...' Tom didn't know what to say. This man terrified him, yet here he was being kind and helpful. 'I...I'm okay, thanks.' Tom couldn't decide if what he had just witnessed was real or not. The vision had such a surreal quality to it that he thought he might have been dreaming.

Mum broke his train of thought. 'Are you sure you're okay?' She still looked concerned but Tom tried his best to reassure her.

'I'm fine. Honest.'

'Well, you take care, Sonny, y'hear? Have an ice cream or something to cool yourself down. I think you need it,' and with that Mr. Lampard was gone.

'Are you sure you're okay?' It was Abi's turn now to fuss around Tom and he didn't like it.

'I'm fine,' he grumped and before anyone could say another word he was on his feet and standing outside on the pavement, but couldn't help wondering why he had a feeling that something wasn't right.

* * *

Deciding to take Mr. Lampard's suggestion, they stopped at *Suggits* for an ice cream. As they licked at their cones, ducks paddled back and forth over the shallow riverbed, the sunlight glinting off the slowly moving water. Abi and Mum settled into a quiet mood but Tom had a sense of being watched. A few times he caught Mum eyeing him and put it down to her concern over him passing out but then it was gone. Once in the car the sensation continued, but Mum and Abi seemed more like themselves by the time they reached home and Tom had soon forgotten about it.

It took Tom a while to convince Mum that he was okay, but, before long, he was climbing over the dry stone wall at the bottom of the garden with his sister, eager to reach the majestic hills and woods beyond. The grass was soft and tufted, growing in thick, coarse clumps, dandelions sprouting along the edge of the wall as it ran downhill towards an old weather-beaten oak tree. The ground rolled gently into a ditch and then steadily up again until another stone wall cut across its path. Tom and Abi climbed through a narrow break in the stones, taking care not to dislodge any as they went, and crossed the narrow railway bridge which spanned the Middlesbrough to Whitby line, before entering the field beyond.

The woods seemed much closer and Tom was eager to be off and explore. He was like a restrained dog on its leash, only held back by his mother's call for him to *take it easy* and *wait for his sister*. He raced ahead a little but stopped after a few hundred metres, panting for breath after his race to the first outcroppings of the wood and sat down. It didn't take long for Abi to catch up and they both looked expectantly at Mum as she strode towards them at a more leisurely pace.

'Go on then, but don't stray too far from each other,' she called out across the distance. 'Abi, keep a close eye on him, okay? And watch out for rabbit holes,' she shouted as they ran towards the trees. 'I don't want any broken ankles.'

Tom raced into the cover. Abi followed more sedately but still made enough noise to frighten any wildlife within a kilometre. She soon found the little stream they always looked for and followed it upwards to its bubbling origins among the rocks.

Moving across soft carpets of pine needles and ever-thickening undergrowth, they found themselves snagged more than once on sharp twigs or bramble thorns. It was as if the wood were trying to prevent them from delving deeper into its heart, trying to dissuade them from discovering a long hidden secret. Finally, after much scrambling, they reached the top of the hill and slumped to the ground, their breathing heavy after their climb. Gazing out, Tom saw the graceful curve of the Tees bay, its blue-grey waters broken by slowly-moving white caps, and the motionless forms of heavily-laden tankers as they waited to unload their cargo at Tees Port. In the distance huge wind turbines spun relentlessly in the summer wind, their white blades cutting through the purple haze of Hartlepool, like a knife through the mist. Tom smiled and laid back on the warm rock: he felt as if he was on top of the world.

Abi broke the silence. 'What happened today?' Tom

knew she had been waiting to ask.

Pausing before answering, Tom composed his answer carefully but ended up muttering a simple reply. 'I think I turned around too quickly, went dizzy and fell over.' He knew it was much more than that but didn't know quite what and didn't want to discuss it any further. Not with his sister. Not now. He sat up and looked at the view again but knew she was still watching him. He stood up.

'Come on.' He took a few steps and looked around to see Abi still sitting there watching him. When he next spoke it wasn't so politely. 'Come *on!*'

* * *

Nearly two hours later, knees, bottoms and elbows coated with generous layers of mud and faces like those of commandos hiding out in the jungle, two tired and hungry but very happy children emerged from the dappled cover of the wood.

They smiled a bit sheepishly at each other as they approached their Mum who dozed in the warm sunshine, her sketchpad openly discarded as the warmth of the day had lulled her into a peaceful slumber.

Opening one eye at the sound of movement, she looked from Abi to Tom, then back again.

'Look at the state of you two,' she chuckled.

Tom and Abi giggled. 'What?' asked Tom, feigning innocence.

'You know,' Mum replied, climbing to her feet. 'You'll just have time for a bath before your father gets home. Not that he'll mind, I'm sure.' She waved her hand at them dismissively. 'Go on with you.'

Abi smiled. 'Race you!' she squealed and set off down

the hill, Tom following behind at a galloping pace, his longer legs soon eating up the distance between them.

'Hey! That's not fair! You didn't warn me!' called Mum after them, but it was too late. They crossed the bridge and reached the gap in the wall, slowing only enough to climb through without hurting themselves. Abi was still in the lead, when Mum looked up from collecting her pad and pencils, but Tom was right on her heels.

Deciding it was too hot to run, Mum stood with her face turned up to the sun. Its rays gently warmed her face, and she sighed at the beauty of it before stepping off towards home.

* * *

Abi leant back against her favourite tree in the garden. The oak was old and stood proudly amongst the others, offering shade and coolness from the heat of the day. Tom lay on the grass close by, idly picking the drying mud from his jeans. They talked about their adventure in the woods and laughed over finding Mum asleep in the middle of the field.

Rolling over to face his sister, Tom propped himself up on one elbow. 'Fancy a game of hide and seek?'

'Yeah, good idea.' Abi was on her feet before he could say another word. 'You're it!' she shouted and within seconds was gone. Tom chastised himself for not being quicker. She was *always* doing that!

He closed his eyes and started counting.

'…18…19…20. Coming, ready or not!' Opening his eyes he peered through the low branches of the oak tree and stood still to listen. A bee caught his attention as it buzzed lazily among the colourful petals of the flower bed, and he watched it for a few seconds before it droned away into the distance. Hiding behind the bulk of the tree, he listened again for any sound that might betray his sister's hiding place but was startled by the squeak of the gate. He turned to see it swing open and a figure stagger through.

Tom didn't recognise the visitor but immediately felt concern rather than alarm when he saw how it was hunched over. The figure shuffled along the path, right hand held out towards Tom in a pleading gesture, its face contorted in pain, before collapsing slowly to its knees on the edge of the lawn.

Tom stared at the stranger who was sweating profusely, yet shaking as if frozen in spite of the warmth of the day. Then, slumping to one side, the figure lay unmoving. Tom took a step forwards and immediately knew that something was very wrong. Without taking his eyes off the trembling body he began to shout and, as Abi came hurriedly into view, the alarm in his voice stopped her in her tracks. 'Go get Mum,' he said. 'Go now. Go!'

Abi ran back the way they had come minutes earlier and Tom knelt down, although he didn't know what he was going to do.

Instinctively he reached out to touch the body before him and say something soothing, something to help, but as he did his fingertips brushed lightly against the shirt and he recoiled suddenly as if bitten.

He could feel the intense heat from the body beneath.

The man was burning – he was on fire.

CHAPTER 4

The world was a hazy slow motion dream.

Figures moved as if in a viscous liquid and spoke in heavy, drawn-out voices which merged one with another. They dragged across his vision in a painfully distorted blur, settling into barely recognisable forms as his brain caught up with the movement of his eyes, the sound of their movement clashing like an over-recorded soundtrack within the confines of his head.

He felt himself lifted, carried, dragged, and sensed something soft beneath him. A face loomed into his vision and he recoiled. Dark eyes bored into him but, no matter how hard he willed himself to look away, his body would not respond.

Hands touched him and a sudden coolness covered his body where his skin burned. His flesh seemed to crawl as if contracting, and a tear of pain rolled down his face, its saltiness stinging his flesh as its bitterness wet his lips and the light hurt his eyes.

He was in his own private hell.

Voices continued to drone unintelligibly, noises and shapes around him flickering in and out of his vision. Somehow he knew he was being helped but had no idea of where he was or who was with him. For a moment his tears ceased and he tried to raise his head but was gently pressed back.

A voice spoke.

He looked up once more into dark eyes. In the midst of his pain and disorientation he realised they were not the eyes of the figure he had seen before. These eyes were black, as black as ebony and shining with the reflections of the room around him. They were almond shaped, almost feminine and tilted upwards within a grey face. The head tilted slowly to one side and moved closer. He could hear the slight sound of rasping breathing and smelt something which seemed familiar, yet, at the same time, his muddled brain told him he had never smelt it before.

And the eyes stared the coldest stare he had ever seen.

CHAPTER 5

Mum froze.

For a few seconds she stood with her mouth agape but said nothing.

'He's hot, Mum. I mean *really* hot.' Tom said, his hand hovering a few centimetres above the burning skin.

Mum knelt and looked into the disorientated eyes, her hand resting tentatively on the stranger's shoulder as she did. She recoiled slightly at the intensity of the heat but laid her hand on his shirt again in a reassuring manner.

'Are you all right?' she asked, not really expecting a reply. She raised her voice slightly. 'What's your name?'

The stranger moaned, his eyes moving erratically from side to side as if searching for something. 'He can't stay out here. We've got to get him inside,' said Mum. 'Help me move him.' She struggled to lift his shoulders until he was sitting forward and reached under his armpits, clasping her hands tightly around each other across his chest. She ignored the damp, clammy feel of his shirt and the raging heat beneath. 'Tom, you grab his belt. Abi, you lift his feet over the door step.'

Abi looked scared. 'Mum…' she said in her timid *I don't want to do this* voice, but grabbed his feet by the heels nevertheless. His boots were muddy, the dirt dried on.

'Ready? Okay, lift!'

Mum and Tom lifted together, and with shuffling steps they stumbled into the hallway. Abi did her best but lost her balance, dropped his feet and fell against the dirty trouser legs.

'Ugh!' she cried, feeling the heat for the first time and rebelling against it.

Tom pulled with all his strength, his knuckles wet under the waistband, and staggered into the hall. He released the weight for a brief rest while Abi prepared herself again.

Between them they managed to drag the slumped figure through the doorway to the living room before depositing him, unceremoniously, in an untidy heap. Half on and half off the sofa, he breathed heavily and mumbled incoherently under his breath. Lifting his feet, Abi helped to straighten him and then stepped away.

'We've got to do something about this temperature,' said Mum firmly. 'Tom, Abi, go and get some towels from the bathroom. Soak them under the cold tap. Quick as you can. Go! Go!'

Tom ran but Abi just stood, staring at the dirty and dishevelled figure which lay on the sofa.

'Abi?' Mum asked, waving her hand in front of her eyes. 'Abi? Go and help your brother.' Abi blinked, shook her head as if clearing it and then turned. Without a sound, she ran upstairs and Mum could hear them both banging around, their voices, and the sound of running water, dull through the ceiling above her.

'You're red hot,' said Mum, as much to herself as to the stranger. He squinted up at her, staring into her eyes, as if trying to focus, when suddenly his own went wide.

Digging his heels into the cushions of the sofa, he tried to push himself away. His mouth opened and closed furiously making choking, panicking noises, but he seemed unable to unlock his eyes from those above him. The look of panic gave way to one of terror.

Frightened herself, Mum covered it well as Tom and Abi raced back, towels tracing dark drip patterns across the stone floor.

'Hey, hey, hey…' cooed Mum gently, leaning over the figure, 'it's alright. We only want to help you.' The look of terror on the stranger's face unnerved Mum greatly. *What's happened to him?* she thought. *Why is he reacting like this?*

'Is he alright Mum?' Tom looked worried for the first time. The initial shock of the situation seemed to be wearing off and he was beginning to see the seriousness of the whole thing. But Abi was still silent. She stood a little behind her brother, yet close enough to see what was happening.

'I don't know, but we must cool him down. He can't stay this hot for long, his body won't take it.' Mum unbuttoned the front of his shirt and took a sodden towel from Abi. She draped it over his chest and pressed it to his skin, water dribbling out and soaking into the sofa cushions.

The stranger squirmed in discomfort at the sudden cold and cried out again before settling back onto the sofa. His breathing was heavy and rhythmic but his distress seemed to ease. Mum looked to Abi and held her arm out, motioning for her to cuddle in but Tom stayed where he was.

As they stood, the figure closed his eyes and swallowed hard. A single tear welled and traced its path across his cheek, settling in the corner of his mouth and soaking into his parched lips. Another bout of panic suddenly struck and he screwed up his eyes against the brightness beaming in through the open window, raising his hands to shield himself from the glare.

'We need to close the curtains,' said Tom. 'I think the light is too bright for him.' He took a step towards the sofa and looked at his sister. She didn't respond but then seemed to register what he had said. Without a word, she moved off and the room soon plunged into darkness. For a few seconds it was almost total, but their eyes soon began to adjust, and the scene spread out before them in monochrome.

In his prostrate position, the stranger's breathing began to steady. The sudden shade in the room helped him to settle, but then he lifted his head. Mum stepped forward and pushed him firmly down again, taking the other towel and gently positioned it across the top of his head. 'Hush, now. Lie still,' she said, her tone soothing, but, as she leant over, their eyes locked for a second time.

This time, Mum saw something pass through them that she couldn't place. It was a look so foreign, so unreadable, that it made her shudder.

CHAPTER 6

The sound of a car door slamming broke into the stillness of the room, followed by the garden gate squealing in protest, as it always did. Footsteps crunched down the gravel path and shuffled on the concrete step. A heavy *thump* echoed through the kitchen as something hit the floor hard. 'Anybody home?'

Dad left his toolbox where it was and kicked off his shoes into the under-stair cupboard. Suddenly startled by the sound of crying, he hurried into the living room but stopped in the doorway with a jolt. On the sofa was a figure, wrapped up in what looked like blankets, and it was crying uncontrollably.

Mum stepped towards the door and took Dad to one side, hurriedly explaining what had happened. Abi clung tightly round both their waists while Tom eased himself into a chair with a dazed look on his face.

Left on his own while Mum talked, the stranger began to calm. Dad stood with his arms wrapped around Abi, silent concern etched on his face as he listened, but his eyes never left the figure before him. Slowly disentangling himself from Abi's arms, he pecked her on the head reassuringly and walked over to the sofa. As he knelt down, he could feel the heat radiating from the figure, the towel covering the body almost dry now, but the figure didn't seem to register that Dad was there: he just continued to cry, his vision entranced by his own demons.

'Who is he? What's...?' Dad paused, shuffling back

slightly and looked at Mum before continuing. 'He could be contagious. We don't know what's happened to him.'

Without knowing why he was doing it, Dad found himself reaching out. He paused briefly then lifted the towel from the stranger's head.

A surprised, almost quizzical look spread over his face.

'Well, would you believe it...' he muttered, leaning towards the body for a better look. Mum was concerned that the stranger would react as he had earlier, but he didn't move. He just continued to stare at the ceiling.

'Pete...' she began, not wanting to break the silence which had descended. 'Do you...know him?' Then, after a pause, she repeated, 'Pete?'

'Danny Forbes,' whispered Dad. 'Danny Forbes.' Frightened eyes slowly turned to meet Dad's and the two men looked at each other. Dad saw something in his eyes – something he didn't like.

'What's up, Danny?' asked Dad, quietly. 'What's happened to you?'

Some instinct told Danny who was with him but he couldn't focus enough to respond.

When Dad spoke again, Danny whimpered and curled himself up. He shrunk into the back of the sofa as if stung, trying desperately to protect himself. He seemed unable to cope with anything, even the twisted thoughts that were raging through his mind. Dad touched him lightly and instantly regretted it, shocked for a second time at the heat. Danny screamed, his body twitching and contorting as if trying to escape from something, from somewhere.

Dad chewed his lip thoughtfully as he walked slowly towards Mum and stood beside her, deep in thought. When he eventually spoke, his voice was distant. 'Danny

Forbes and I went to school together. We were the best of friends until we had a falling out over something… something stupid. I haven't seen him for… what…? it must be the best part of twenty years.' Dad whistled softly and shook his head. 'But that's not Danny, at least, not the Danny I knew.' He paused and looked back towards the sofa. 'What's happened?'

Danny lay still, his face a shifting mask of pain and fear.

'What are we going to do, Dad?' Abi spoke for the first time, her voice trembling as she huddled up close again.

'We'll think of something. It'll be alright,' Dad replied soothingly as he stroked her hair and smiled.

Mum gripped Dad's arm. 'He can't stay here, Pete. He needs more help than we can give him.'

Dad nodded in agreement. He moved slowly towards the telephone but stopped, his hand poised above the receiver, when the figure spoke. The single word, barely more than a whisper, cut the air with the intensity of its emotion.

'No.'

Dad turned and was beside his friend in a single step. The word was repeated.

'Danny, you need to talk to me. You've got to tell me what happened. If you want me to help, you've *got* to tell me!'

'Don't put me in hospital. Please.' The voice ended with a long, shuddering intake of breath. 'I'm not contagious. I haven't been infected. Something… something…'

'Something what?' asked Dad, exasperation filling his voice. 'What *happened*, Danny? We *need* to *know!*'

Unconsciousness seemed to engulf the figure but Dad

grabbed him roughly by the shoulders and shook. 'Danny!' he called out, louder than he planned to. 'Danny,' he repeated, more quietly this time. 'Come on, Danny. What happened to you?' Dad sat on the edge of the sofa and waited.

Danny's eyes looked around the room, but appeared as though blind. Finally, they focussed. Both men looked at each other, and then it was Dad's turn to be in pain – the painful dilemma of wanting to help his former friend, yet at the same time needing to protect his family.

'What happened to you, Danny?'

Danny saw at last who was with him. 'Oh, Pete.' He dissolved into racking sobs again.

Dad turned quietly to mum. 'Take the kids outside, Debs. It might be best.' Mum nodded, ushered Tom and Abi through the door and closed it quietly behind them.

The crying slowly subsided and the room was quiet, disturbed only by the sound of the clock ticking softly on the mantelpiece.

'What happened, Danny? What happened?'

'I...I...don't know,' Danny mumbled quietly after a pause. 'Something...it...' A long pause followed and Dad thought he had drifted into unconsciousness again, but the voice continued. 'I don't know.' He looked at Dad with a sorrowful, lost expression, tears welling again behind his eyes. Dad would later describe it as the look someone might have if they had lost part of their life – *really* lost it, he would say – as if it had been cut or ripped away.

'You need to go to the hospital,' said Dad. 'It's the best place for you. It's the safest for everyone. You don't know you're not contagious and I've got to think of Debbie and the kids. You know that, Danny. Look at you, you're a wreck.'

Danny reached up with his right hand and grabbed Dad's shirt sleeve. Dad could feel the heat.

'Please, Pete, don't call them. I tell you, I'm not contagious.' He sounded desperate.

'How do you know? You said yourself you don't remember what happened. That really doesn't fill me with confidence.'

'I know, I know, but please, you've got to trust me.' He sounded tired now and his voice was weakening.

'We go back a long way, Danny, but I don't know if I can help you out with this.'

Both men paused. Danny gripped Dad's sleeve tighter and fixed him with a vacant stare. He whispered with all the strength he could manage.

'My head's a mess. I don't know....' He started to cough. When he finished, he looked back at Dad, his voice muffled and barely audible. 'It's different this time, Pete. It's different.'

Dad froze, a chill of familiarity running through his body. 'What do you mean, it's different? What's different?'

Dad shook him again, hard this time.

'Danny! What's different?'

But Danny could no longer answer.

Over the next hour the heat from Danny's body lessened. He wasn't sweating as much, but his sleep remained troubled.

Dad sat watching the exhausted figure, thinking back to his youth and the times Danny and he had shared. He remembered with anguish why they had fallen out and sighed heavily.

It had been over something and nothing. Something silly that Dad hadn't been able to accept but Danny was obsessed with, yet nothing worth losing a good friendship over. Looking back now, Dad realised that he had been foolish.

A true friend would have stuck by and helped when it was needed, but what had he done? He'd walked away because other people didn't understand what Danny had been through and had judged him because of it. They'd called him "strange", said he was "a bit weird", and Dad hadn't wanted to be judged in the same way. In the end he'd been too young to realise that friendship was a bond stronger than words. He'd been too young to understand fully what it meant to stand up and help someone, and had broken their bond.

It wasn't the first time he had felt guilty in the years since, but he hadn't known where to find Danny. Even if he had, he wouldn't have known how to make it up anyway. But now he had a chance to make amends: he had an opportunity to put things right.

Somehow Dad knew that Danny was telling the truth, and that whatever had happened to him was not dangerous. He didn't know *how* he knew, but somehow he did.

Danny's final words echoed inside his head. *It's different this time, Pete.*

It's different.

What was different? What did he mean?

A familiar feeling came over Dad and he shuddered.

Not again! Oh, please, not again!

CHAPTER 7

The Old Vicarage nestled quietly into the countryside at the top of the village. Its east facing windows took in views of rolling landscape, thickly wooded plantations and dotted farmhouses, while the northern outlook glimpsed the village green and houses beyond. The Village Hall and General Dealers sat to one side of the green, its lone tree standing proud against the summer sky, the single bus stop and bench below dwarfed by the immense size of its roots and canopy. Behind the Old Vicarage, the crumbling road gave way to a dirt track, and, beyond the dry stone walls, the landscape of the Cleveland hills unfolded.

To the people of Northern England the high vantage points and open moors were a beauty which stretched out from their doorstep, entwined with a rich history of towns, people and events from days gone by. Walkers regularly streamed over the well-trodden footpaths and bridleways that rambled their way through the heather and bracken, their routes taking in historical sites and outstanding viewpoints: Roseberry Topping, an ancient up-thrust of sandstone capped rock; Captain Cook's Monument, named for the 18th Century explorer who was born in Marton and sailed out of Whitby; and Pin Point, standing proud above the village of Carlton in Cleveland.

A little to the north of Roseberry Topping the Cleveland hills rose once again as they spread towards the coast. Atop them a solitary finger pointed towards the sky, a lone monument to the early Bronze and Iron Age settlements of Eston Nab.

For nearly a hundred years the hills had almost single-handedly shaped the history of the local area. In 1850 ironstone was discovered and an industry burst into life which still resonated through the area decades after its demise. A labyrinth of tunnels ran deep into the hillside while railway lines crisscrossed their way from the pit tops to Cargo Fleet, bringing out more than 63 million tons of ironstone throughout the ninety-nine years of their life. Whole communities had swiftly sprung up to support the workers and their families, and those communities still echoed with pride long afterwards.

But eventually Mother Earth was picked dry of her spoils, and the hills were all but exhausted, bringing the age of Eston ironstone mining to a close. With much sorrow the mineshafts were sealed and the railways dismantled, but the rivers and springs continued to run as red as rust, a reminder of what once was.

Tranquillity returned to the hillsides and the mines finally settled into silence. Sealed and forgotten, the days of their history lengthened and none but a few gave thought to their existence.

And that made them the perfect place to hide.

CHAPTER 8

The summer sun shone directly in through the open kitchen door, dust floating lazily in its warm rays. Outside the day seemed perfect but the atmosphere inside had changed.

Mum had shooed Tom and Abi upstairs, telling them to stay there. Now they squatted on the staircase trying to hear what was being said beyond the kitchen door. Occasionally there were the sounds of raised voices or the clink of cups, but ultimately nothing that told them what was going on.

'What do you think's going to happen?' Abi asked quietly.

'Dunno.' Tom relied absently, desperately trying to listen, irritated by his sister's interruptions. 'Anyway, shush! I can't hear!'

'I don't like him. He scares me,' Abi said after a pause. She shuddered and folded her arms tightly across her chest.

Tom didn't answer; he just pressed his head tighter against the spindles of the staircase.

They sat quietly for a few minutes, neither of them moving, before Abi whispered. Tom shushed her again but she continued. Distracted, Tom turned and saw Abi was sitting with her eyes closed, her lips moving silently.

'What are you doing?' he whispered. For a few seconds she didn't move, and then her eyes snapped open. Tom didn't like it. He instantly felt like some kind of specimen under a microscope, but before he could say anything Abi climbed quietly to her feet and crept up the stairs towards her bedroom.

Tom felt his whole body tremble, the feeling of being watched unsettling him, but tried his best to push the sensation from his mind.

He turned slowly back to his eavesdropping, but it was nearly an hour before anything happened.

* * *

Mum and Dad had struggled to come to an agreement, but Dad had finally managed to convince Mum that everything would be okay. She just hoped she wouldn't regret it later.

Mum was worried. She knew something had happened with Danny a long time ago and her husband now felt compelled to help his friend, but, no matter how many times she'd asked, Dad had refused to say any more. He'd said that it was ancient history – *water under the bridge*. It wasn't something he could discuss and he wouldn't be drawn any further. It made Mum's insides churn.

Dad stood up and poured their cold cups of tea down the sink. Making them had been an excuse to get up and move around when the conversation had been difficult. Neither had really wanted the drink in the first place

'Right. I'll go and make up the spare bed,' said Mum reluctantly. Dad mumbled agreement and walked towards the living room door. There hadn't been a sound from the other room for the whole time they'd been in the kitchen.

Dad peered inside. The sleeping figure of Danny now slumbered peacefully, the towels that had soaked him earlier lay heaped on the floor and his left arm draped across his forehead.

Picking up the towels, Dad placed them on the back of the sofa before walking over to the fireplace and staring at his own reflection in the mirror. He tried to remember what he had looked like nearly twenty years ago, when he and Danny had still been friends. His hair had been longer then – a *lot* longer – and he smiled at the memory. He'd been younger, thinner, and ready to take on the world. Full of raw energy and enthusiasm, but the world had been much harder to deal with than he'd imagined.

He'd had his knocks but had learnt to *roll with the punches*, as his Dad used to say. His Dad had been right about a good many things and he wished he'd listened to the advice he'd been given. *You think you know it all*, his Dad had said on many an occasion. He'd still had a great deal to learn and his Dad's advice had been sound.

If only I'd listened. Sorting out his friendship with Danny should have been at the top of the list.

He glanced at the clock. Ten past four. Was it that time already? He'd finished work early today as he had planned to do some jobs around the house, work on those things that needed a bit of attention but always seemed to get away from him, but now the afternoon had been frittered away.

Danny mumbled in his sleep and Dad sat on the edge of the sofa. Sometime during the course of the afternoon Danny's watch must have spun around on his wrist and was now staring Dad in the face. Something seemed wrong but he couldn't put his finger on it. He stared at the watch for a few seconds and, with a blast of recognition, it struck him.

The watch was exactly one hour slow.

CHAPTER 9

Deep inside the mine shafts, under the cracked and buckling roof supports of another time, it silently carried out its task.

It watched.

It listened.

It sensed.

It made no noise, gave no indication of its presence and kept its origins hidden. Its makers had created and educated the Searcher before sending it on its way. Now it sat quietly within Mother… and waited.

A change was sensed. The slightest variation in its readings identified.

Mother spoke and a decision was made.

Without a sound, and without warning, Mother shot vertically upwards at incredible speed. Rocks, earth and wooden supports were unable to hold her and she punched through them, like a bullet through a paper bag, sending a plume of earth high into the night. Splintered timbers fell back to the floor of the tunnel and dust hung in thick clouds as the collapsed tunnel settled into silence, the air swirling in descending eddies.

A few metres above the shaft, Mother came to an abrupt halt. She paused until all was ready, and then Searcher was born into the world of humans.

Searcher rose quickly until it came to hover ten metres above the hillside, then gave a single pulse of silver light and floated silently towards the sleeping village.

CHAPTER 10

The illuminated red figures of the digital clock cast an eerie glow across the room. Seconds slipped into minutes and minutes into hours, unnoticed by the sleeping figure.

2:46

2:47

Dreams, fitful and unwanted, invaded his sleep. His mind swirled and threw one image into another in a kaleidoscope of colour and shape before finally settling into less disorientating patterns. A shadowy figure disturbed him and he stirred several times, calling out from the depths of his sleep, but each time settled again without waking.

3:01

3:02

His eyes flew open, but he did not wake. Danny stared sightlessly at the ceiling, aware only of a red glow in the darkness before closing once more to slip back into the troubled depths of his mind.

Images continued to batter his subconscious and he shook his head as if to clear it. At one point his arms came up suddenly, shielding himself from some unseen enemy before slipping back, the visions subsiding.

3:23

3:24

Discomfort grew and in the depths of his mind he felt a rising dread. A dread which approached from the depths of his mind. A dread from which he could not wake.

The feeling of foreboding increased, its tendrils reaching out, probing, like the legs of a spider sensing their way across the unfamiliar territory of his mind.

Through his bedroom wall Tom heard strange noises and mumbled sleep-talking which increased as the night drew on. He lay in the darkness, willing sleep to come, yet not wanting to close his eyes. Eventually he dozed, but when he glanced at the clock, staring at him across the darkness of his room, he found only minutes had passed.

As he at last fell into a deep sleep, he was suddenly woken by a deafening scream.

* * *

Dark eyes. Peering. Searching. Boring into his mind. Danny awoke with a start, his throat raw and dry. He sat bolt upright in bed, his shirt glued to his body in a sheen of perspiration and swung his legs over the side of the bed, needing to feel the solid floor beneath his feet. He needed to know he was awake.

Where am I?

He looked into the dark shadows thrown by unfamiliar furniture, into a room he didn't know.

The curtains fluttered in the breeze from the open window, its coolness refreshing. He stood up and took a tentative step towards the centre of the room. Then it all came flooding back: where he was, in whose home he was sleeping, and somehow he felt a little better. Reassured. He shivered but was not cold.

He remembered something, something which

disturbed his mind, jolted it hard and the dread returned like a painful explosion.

Light. Bright and blinding.

A sense of being held. Restrained.

The most worrying visions came next, cascading into his brain and tumbling over each other in an effort to be let out. Visions of events and their ultimate connection.

He suddenly understood what had been happening, what had been going on for all those years, and it frightened him. It frightened him badly.

His brain dredged up more and deposited it in front of him: rocky ground bleached by the hot sun, a wide open desert cut by long gouges which ripped up the earth until they ended abruptly, charred and burnt.

Something shone, reflecting the bright sunlight in his mind.

Silver, he thought.

Foil? No, not foil. Something else.

He couldn't see it clearly but knew it shouldn't be there. His mind flashed again and he saw curved linear forms, smooth, twisted and tortured, then something small, unknown, yet, at the same time, strangely familiar poking from the wind blown ground. Although he tried he couldn't focus his mind clearly enough to see, but knew that whatever it was, it was totally out of place.

His mind shifted abruptly, the images moving, changing.

Somewhere else now. Dark. Cold. Silent.

Tall forms emerged from the cloudiness of his mind.

Blinding lights.

Sudden movement.

Hiding?

Running?

What was it?

He saw a myriad of piercing white lights moving in formation, *but what were they?*

The lights dimmed to become black and shiny, their shape changing to sweep upwards, almond like. And they stared. They stared hard.

'Return.'

Danny yelped. The word had been felt rather than heard – felt somewhere inside the inner workings of his brain.

'Return.'

He jerked back with a start and ended up sprawled on the bed, gasping for breath and shaking, his chest shuddering as he forced oxygen into his lungs and began to cough once more. His whole body was racked and he felt his consciousness begin to slip.

The world went dark and in his slide he felt hands restraining him, gripping him firmly.

He couldn't move.

CHAPTER 11

Tom opened his door just enough to peer through, his face a mask of worry as he listened to the voices beyond.

Dad had grabbed Danny as he fell from the bed, catching him just in time before he ended up in a heap on the floor.

Danny mumbled and opened his eyes. 'Uhn! Where…?' He vaguely remembered what had happened.

Everything went quiet again. Dad's voice floated out to Mum who now stood with her arms around Abi.

'Can you get me a glass of water?' Abi flinched at Dad's question and gripped tighter, not wanting to let Mum go.

'It'll be alright,' Mum whispered. 'I'm only going to the bathroom. You want to come with me?' Abi nodded and Mum looked at Tom, her eyebrows raised in question, but he shook his head. Mum set off down the landing, Abi shadowing her.

Tom heard the clink of a glass against the sink as Mum filled it, then movement as she returned. As she wafted past, her white cotton dressing gown flowed open from the hastily-tied belt around her waist and Tom was struck by how pale her legs looked against the darkness. 'Stay here,' said Mum before stepping into the room. Abi stood at the door but didn't venture any further.

The light switch made a loud *click* in the darkness and Tom jumped, sensitive to every sound. He squinted into the yellow beam that sprang from the open doorway and slowly opened his own door a little more. He felt his confidence growing now that Mum and Dad were both in there.

Dad spoke. 'Here, have a drink.' Tom heard the water being gulped down, then Dad's voice again. 'Woa! Steady! Steady!'

A choking cough and the sound of someone gasping for air flooded onto the landing and Tom found himself moving closer to his sister. They glanced at each other and then into the room.

Danny lay against the side of the bed, the quilt in a dishevelled heap on the floor beside him. The empty glass, still in his hand, was tipped over as Danny held the back of his hand against his mouth. He coughed again.

'Right. Let's have you up,' said Dad. He passed the glass to Mum and with a heave Danny collapsed unceremoniously onto the bed.

Danny took a couple of deep breaths. 'I'm sorry,' he said quietly then looked up and caught sight of Tom and Abi silhouetted in the light from the landing. 'I'm so, so sorry,' he repeated. 'I must have scared you two half to death.' Danny looked down at his hands before burying his face in them. 'The dreams…the dreams,' he mumbled and sniffed, shaking his head as he took a big breath to try and steady himself.

'What's this all about?' asked Dad after a pause. He sat on the bed and put his hand on Danny's shoulder. It felt slightly warm but nothing like it had been hours earlier. 'What's going on?'

Danny turned towards Dad and sighed. 'You'll think I've lost it. You'll think I've cracked.'

'Hey, we've known each other for…well… a long time.' He paused then went on. 'I know I didn't do the right thing by you before – I know I wasn't there for you – but I've had time to do a lot of thinking over the years and I know you wouldn't be here now if you didn't have good reason.' Dad looked Danny straight in the eye. 'Come on, mate. Tell me what's been happening.'

'You're not going to believe it. Even after what happened when we were kids, you're not going believe it.' Dad frowned and Danny waited for him to speak. When he didn't, Danny continued.

'I don't know where to start…I mean, it's so …'

Dad's voice was quiet, calming. 'Tell me what you remember.'

'Are you sure you want to hear this? It's going to sound really strange, weird even.'

'Go on.'

Danny thought for a moment. 'Do you remember when we were kids, how we played up on the hills and nothing we did seemed to have any consequence?'

'Mm-hm.'

'How everything seemed to happen… just because it did?'

Dad nodded.

'Well, what if I told you it didn't happen *just* because it did?'

Dad looked confused and Mum sat on the bed beside him. She wrapped her dressing gown more tightly around her legs but didn't say anything.

'What do you mean, *just* because it did?'

'I mean, we played the games we wanted to, went where we wanted to and nothing seemed to stop us. We always thought the world was ours. Ours to do with as we wanted...'

'We were kids,' laughed Dad.

'I know we were kids, but we didn't seem to see any danger, did we?'

'You didn't,' laughed Dad. 'I remember the time we built that tarzee, the rope swing in the tree at the old Brickworks, do you remember? You climbed up to tie the rope on, and I mean *up*.' Dad turned to Mum. 'The tree grew out over a drop which must have been what? four or five metres?' He looked back at Danny for confirmation before returning to Mum. 'I didn't dare do it. It was way too high for me, but him, he climbed up there like a monkey and shinned along the branch without any fear at all. When he'd tied the rope he swung under the branch and just hung there, laughing his head off.'

Danny managed a small smile at the memory, but his mind was elsewhere and he couldn't shake the dark thoughts that stirred inside his head.

Dad continued. 'And then he let go. He just...let go! He seemed to take forever to hit the ground, and when he did I thought he would break every bone in his body.'

'What happened?' Mum spoke for the first time.

'It was that hot summer of '76. We'd been baking for weeks but the mud was still quite soft in places where the tree cover had been its thickest. Only I didn't know just *how* wet, and this so-and-so hadn't *told* me!'

Danny laughed.

'He'd been up there and planned it all without me. The top layer of mud had gone hard but was really quite thin, so when he hit it he went right through and ended up in mud up to his knees.' Dad accentuated the event by drawing his hands across his knees in a sawing motion. 'I could have killed him!' said Dad, 'but I had the last laugh because no matter how hard he tried he couldn't get out. The mud was so thick it was like standing inside two tubes. He ended up flat on his back with all the wriggling and lost both trainers into the bargain!'

'Yeah, I walked home in my socks and my Mum went mad,' added Danny. 'She grounded me for the rest of the holidays, but I drove her nuts within a week and she let me off.'

Both men looked at each other and smiled at the memory, but Danny's smile soon faded. 'That was when we were kids, but it's all changed now. Believe me, it's all changed.' His voice was shaking.

'What do you mean?' asked Dad, his smile gone as well.

'It's not even like it for them anymore,' said Danny, gesturing towards the two figures in the doorway.

'Hey, we all know the world's changed, and not necessarily for the better. Okay, maybe it's not as safe as it once was and you have to watch your back a lot more, but it's not that bad.' Dad sat with a serious look on his face.

'It's not watching your back I'm talking about. It's not watching each other, it's...' Danny stumbled to find the words and nervousness descended over him again.

'What are you talking about?' asked Mum, joining in the conversation.

'It's not us we need to worry about,' said Danny.

'What do you mean, it's not us?'

'Us. The human race.'

Dad looked worried. He remembered the past only too well. 'Danny...is this going where I *think* its going?' he asked worriedly.

Danny stood up. 'You haven't changed! You're still thinking the same as you did back then!'

'No, no, I'm not. I'm not. Look, I know what I did was wrong; I should have stood by you and helped you when you needed support. I may not accept or believe what you believe but I'm not going to turn away from you again. Not this time.'

'It's different this time. I promise.' He stood up and faced Danny. 'I just need to know where this whole thing is going, what I'm going to have to deal with'

He took his friend by the shoulder. Danny flinched and stepped back then slowly sat down, his eyes downcast. It was a while before he spoke. 'Okay,' he said quietly. 'Okay.' His eyes didn't leave his hands, twisting and turning in his lap like spaghetti.

Tom broke the silence. 'What was it you fell out over?'

Danny's hands ceased their fidgeting and he looked at Tom, opening his mouth to answer, but Dad beat him to it.

'Life,' he said.

'Life?' Tom looked puzzled. So did Abi. Mum looked bewildered.

It was Danny's turn to answer. He spoke slowly, quietly, as if he were very carefully measuring his words. 'We fell

47

out over life.' Dad threw a cautious glance at Danny as if trying to gauge what his next reaction was going to be, but he wasn't looking. 'But not ours,' he finished.

Mum looked at both men in confusion. 'So whose life are you talking about?' She turned fully round to face Danny, her body language suddenly defensive as if she didn't want to hear what was coming next.

Danny opened and closed his mouth several times but no sound came. He shook his head slowly and dropped his frightened eyes to stare blankly at the floor.

Mum looked at Dad for some sort of help, some sort of clarification, but his eyes gave a clear message: *don't ask me. Just don't ask me.*

Mum felt the hairs on the back of her neck begin to stand up.

CHAPTER 12

The night was dark and, without a moon to light the way, the paths across the hillside were difficult to navigate. The uneven surface frequently caused careless walkers to stumble, but the Searcher needed neither light nor clear paths to find its way.

Floating across the landscape it hovered a few metres above the dry grass like a dimly glowing torch, then dipped silently into a shallow ravine where it paused before changing direction. As if sniffing the air it confirmed its direction and distance, then accelerated once more. Heading towards a small cluster of yellow lights, it drew close, singled out a shadow silhouetted against the darkness of the hillside, and slowed. Its inner light pulsed briefly as once again it threw open a net of sensors and waited a millionth of a second for the signal to be returned. To the Searcher it was an eternity, but the signal eventually came and the Searcher drifted towards the edge of the shadow like a predator stalking its prey.

A light in the window came on unexpectedly, bright in the darkness, and the Searcher dropped quickly to the ground. Its own light dimmed to a barely visible glow as it lay in the grass waiting, listening. Satisfied it had not been compromised, it rose slowly, its light remaining dim. Pausing for a few seconds, it made a final sweep of its surroundings before floating towards the curtained window.

Mum shivered. She sat on the edge of the bed attempting to quell the feeling of unease which had appeared like a rock in her stomach. The hairs on the back of her neck prickled and she didn't like it. Something felt very wrong.

She rose hurriedly and walked over to Tom and Abi. They stood in the doorway, not understanding what they had just heard, watching the trio of adults.

'What's going on, Mum?' asked Abi. 'What's wrong?'

'Nothing. Nothing at all. Now you be a good girl and run along to bed. You too Tom.' She smiled, but neither Tom nor Abi believed the smile. They wanted to know what was going on.

As Mum ushered them onto the landing, a voice shouted in alarm. Dad jumped away from the bed and Danny looked up in surprise before stumbling, tangling his feet around themselves and ending up in a startled heap.

The pocket of Danny's trousers had started to smoke and smoulder. Fumes curled upwards, patterns twisting in the air before thinning out and vanishing, leaving a cloying, heavy smell of burning. As the fabric smouldered, three spinning spheres the size of marbles rose silently. At the heart of each was an intense light, brilliantly piercing, illuminating the room in a dazzling glow. The lights pulsated rapidly.

Mum screamed and hugged Tom and Abi tightly to her. She backed quickly out of the room until they were pressed up against the far wall of the landing. Abi was crying but Tom felt entranced: he was drawn to the spheres and wanted to touch them. Somehow he felt a longing to reach out, an emotion stronger than anything he had ever felt before. Slowly he stretched out a hand and one of the spheres drifted towards him but stopped in the doorway. Without thinking, Tom took a step forwards before Mum grabbed him.

'No! Don't!' She grabbed his T-shirt and reeled him back, but he strained against it. He desperately wanted to touch the spheres.

The spheres rose and fell gently like a toy boat on the ocean, and Tom sensed they were waiting to see what he did next. He reached his hand out further until it was directly beneath the nearest sphere.

For an instant his world seemed dislocated, splintered, as if it belonged to someone else, as if he wasn't in his own consciousness but was observing his world from a distance. The slightest sensation of movement, a tickling, like the legs of an insect on the back of his hand, made him aware of an intrusion. It was as if there was something inside his head, something that shouldn't be there. But it continued. Looking. Seeking. Burrowing. He tried to look deeper, tried to see what it was but couldn't focus fully. And then he blinked and it was gone.

The spheres quickly pulled back and began to circle each other while the third drifted away from Tom and joined them. The silence of the room was suddenly shattered by a piercing, high-pitched squeal which rose upwards until it disappeared beyond the range of human hearing.

And then silence.

It was pure luck that kept the splinters of glass from hitting someone as the window exploded. Turned as they were to watch the spheres, Danny and Dad were sheltered from the worst of the blast as the glass scattered across the room, coating everything with a twinkling carpet of razor-sharp fragments. Mum stood in the doorway with Tom and Abi, the flying shards narrowly missing them as the explosion hit the room. Mum had covered Abi with her own body, expecting her back to be cut by a thousand tiny daggers but had been unable to help Tom, yet miraculously he was unharmed. The glass had blown past him, missing his face by centimetres and causing the air around him to swirl like a miniature storm.

A pulsing drone filled the stillness of the room, its low sound heavy and leaden. A brilliant light, its beam sharp and piercing, caused the glass shards scattered across the room to glitter like tiny stars as they reflected the light in a million directions. And then a burning blue-white ball, crackling with energy slipped through the space once occupied by the window. Parting the curtains like an actor entering a stage, it moved slowly to hover in the centre of the room.

The spheres moved to encircle the visitor in gradually decreasing orbits until they were absorbed, disappearing with a final crackle. Then, making a slow turn as if surveying the room, the shining orb started towards Danny. He backed away, a look of terror on his face as his sobs of panic dissolved into screams of fear.

The glowing ball hung for what seemed like an eternity, its surface crackling with ferocity and its light almost blinding.

Nobody moved.

CHAPTER 13

Bill Crawford's computer sounded an alert. The alarm blared, stark and abrasive against the soft background hum of the room but was a welcome contrast to the routine of the day. Silencing the alarm with a firm stab, his tiredness was suddenly a thing of the past.

'Right. What have we got?' He spoke softly to himself as he tapped at his monitor. A myriad of symbols scrolled gracefully across the screen. Everything looked normal: satellites followed their graceful arc as they sped around the earth at thousands of kilometres an hour while the International Space Station floated majestically 400 kilometres overhead. Even the departing Space Shuttle *Discovery*, returning its precious cargo of Astronauts and equipment to earth, was right where it was supposed to be.

But something had alerted Fylingdales's computers as

they relentlessly trawled the sky. Something was intruding at the very limits of their range and they had seen it instantly.

A countdown appeared on Bill's screen, ticking away the seconds as he tapped at his keyboard. As part of the Space Surveillance Network, Fylingdales had access to information on every type of spacecraft, aircraft and missile system in the world, yet nothing matched the characteristics of the intruder which currently blinked at him.

The door to the operations room opened and three uniformed figures entered at a sprint. Smithson was the first to reach Bill's station.

'What have you got?' Smithson's American accent was clipped and business-like as he slid into a chair, plugged himself into the console and hurriedly reviewed the data scrolling before him.

'Don't know, sir. It's not coming up as anything we know.' Smithson frowned and tapped the screen. New data appeared.

Two minutes and twenty seconds.

Bill's console began communicating with NORAD, the North American Aero Defence Command hidden deep inside Cheyenne Mountain in Colorado. Long seconds ticked by as the computers ran through their vast data bases, cross-checking the possibilities until a definitive conclusion was reached: NORAD could not identify it. The only thing they were in agreement on was that it wasn't a ballistic missile.

Sixty seconds.

Well, that's something. Bill wiped away the sweat that has formed on his top lip and massaged the knot which had appeared in the back of his neck.

'Sir...?' Bill turned to his Commanding officer, waiting for confirmation to proceed. Time was rapidly disappearing and they only had forty seconds left before a decision had to be made: was it friend or foe? That very decision would start the ball rolling in a succession of events which could affect the whole world. And if it were a wrong decision? By now the object had dropped slightly. It was also changing course as if guiding itself. When it had first been detected it had been high over eastern Europe but now it was moving west.

Thirty seconds.

'Sir...?'

Ten seconds.

Nine.

Eight.

'We need more data, Bill. It doesn't look like an incoming missile. It doesn't match the profile. And look at this: it didn't originate from the surface, it's descending from altitude. If it had been launched from the surface we'd have known.'

The timer reached zero and beeped furiously. Bill silenced it.

'Could it be some space debris we've never recorded before? Something from the Apollo days? Apollo 13, maybe? The explosion blew panels clean off the service module. Perhaps they've finally caught up with us.'

'After thirty years?' John Parlor spoke up for the first time. He'd been looking over Bill's shoulder and trying to make his own sense of what was happening. 'They'd have drifted well out of earth's orbit by now. Anyway, it's changing trajectory. Debris doesn't do that.'

In the past few seconds it had made a distinct change in course and was now headed directly towards the UK.

'At the rate it's descending...' John reached over and tapped the screen – a new menu dropped down. Three more taps and an estimated time of arrival appeared, '...it'll be in UK airspace in just over thirteen minutes.'

Bill chewed his lip.

'We know it's not a missle, and we know it didn't originate on the surface,' said Smithson. 'It'll soon be out of our range. We've got to hand it over.' He picked up a headset. 'I'm transferring to High Wycombe.'

Bill began typing on his keyboard, downloading data to RAF Strike Command in Buckinghamshire. The Duty Controller there would make the final decision whether or not to launch aircraft to intercept.

From that moment on the situation was out of their hands.

* * *

Within minutes two GR1 Tornados were roaring into the sky, scrambled from a base along the East coast. They climbed quickly and banked out over the North Sea, intending to loop around the object, observe and report back before being instructed whether or not to intercept.

It was nothing new. It had happened more times than Bill Crawford or his commanding officer could count, *and no doubt it will happen again*, he thought as he watched two new blips join the masses already on his screen, *but this time something is amiss. It doesn't add up.*

Bill sat back and waited. *By the time the aircraft arrive the target has usually gone or identified itself as something explainable.* He snorted to himself. *It's probably just another satellite slipped out orbit.*

On many occasions the objects disappeared before the fighters could reach them, but on rare occasions the pilots had witnessed things they could not explain, objects which moved with such speed and agility that they vanished within seconds.

Bill watched his screen as the object continued its course, now descending into the mid-layers of the atmosphere. Still over Europe, his computer made continuous calculations of the speed and trajectory of the object and Bill frowned. Maybe it was something of concern after all.

The object would enter UK airspace within the next three minutes and the two fighters, now travelling at the speed of sound, gained on the object with ease.

Two new blips appeared on his screen, their call signs trailing them as they tracked across the map to join the first two aircraft which were now approaching from behind.

The object's rate of descent had remained constant throughout and the aircraft were now within range. Following a well-rehearsed manoeuvre, they split to fly either side… and then it was gone.

With blinding speed it re-appeared directly over the north of England.

'Nothing can do that!' Bill Crawford and his Commanding Officer stared at each other, eyes wide, mouths open in disbelief. Neither could believe what they had just witnessed. They looked at the screen again to double check the data and saw the object was now descending vertically.

Fresh fighters were scrambled, their engines pushing

them to their limits in a race to intercept, but by the time they reached the location the target was going to be on the ground.

Parlor hurried to another console and began flicking switches. The target was about to disappear below the range of their screens and they had to see what was happening.

Bill Crawford shuffled uncomfortably in his seat, feeling the sweat run between his shoulder blades, and looked at his hands. He found they were shaking.

CHAPTER 14

The Searcher hovered, crackling and buzzing like a small electrical storm. It was motionless for long seconds before drifting towards the window. Emitting a sudden high-pitched shriek everyone clamped their hands to their ears, the sound cutting through them like a needle.

A deep droning, more felt than heard, crept into the air. Dad sensed it first and looked up at the window but could see nothing.

'You feel that?' whispered Dad, hardly daring to make a sound.

The Searcher didn't move and Dad stole another quick glance at Mum who still stood shielding Abi. His eyes focused briefly on the digital clock by the side of the bed.

3:42

'Pete, I'm scared.' Mum's voice trembled like a child's and Dad decided he had to get to his family. He looked down at the carpet and saw it was covered in a sheen of glass which extended to the far wall and covered the bed. How was he going to get out here without cutting his feet to shreds? He slipped his dressing gown from his shoulders and threw it against the skirting board, covering the glass splinters lying there.

'Danny,' Dad whispered. 'Danny!'

Danny opened his eyes and slowly turned his head. The look on his face said, *I don't want to move from here. I can't.* He looked petrified.

'Come on.' Dad took a step to his right, his eyes never

leaving the Searcher. He took another. Reaching out he grabbed Danny by his arm and began pulling him. They were nearly half way along the wall.

Mum pushed Abi onto the landing and told her to stay there before stepping back into the doorway but Abi seemed not to hear, her eyes intently watching the visitor. She seemed entranced, whispering silently to herself, her crying now a thing of the past.

Both men froze as the Searcher shifted its position. It spun on the spot as if surveying the room again and Mum took a sharp intake of breath. Danny and Dad crouched, waiting until its movement ceased again before edging another few steps to their right and sliding around the door frame. The look of relief on their faces was obvious.

Dad dropped to his knees and hugged Abi, her trance breaking as he wrapped his arms around her. She jumped and dissolved into floods of tears once again. Dad spent a few seconds trying to cajole her into a smile before turning to Tom.

Tom couldn't take his eyes off the floating object. He was mesmerised. 'It came to me, Dad. It came right up to me. Did you see it? Did you see it?'

'I saw, but come away. I don't want you anywhere near it. It could be dangerous. You hear me?'

Danny stood with his back pressed against the wall, sweat soaking his T-shirt. He looked around nervously, unable to speak. He seemed to feel the rising noise more than the others, the thick carpet beneath their feet shielding them slightly, but now the whole house seemed to be shaking from within. It was frighteningly familiar.

Abi's tiny voice cut through the increasing drone. 'Dad, I don't like this.' She looked up with pleading eyes and pulled at his T-shirt. 'Please, Dad…'

'Let's get away from here.' Mum began moving and everyone else followed. Desperate to escape what was behind them they quickly clattering to the bottom of the stairs. Within seconds the house was jumping as if alive, vibration running through the very foundations, the air humming against their faces. Dust rose, disturbed from the cracks of the old walls and floor to swirl around in the control of some strange force. Ornaments shuffled and clattered on the unit by the front door and a figurine of a Victorian lady slid to the floor and smashed, the noise inaudible against the pounding in their ears. Photograph frames jostled and bumped each other in a wild dance. Without warning the hall light flickered and went out.

Mum screamed, her voice full of panic and Abi clung to her, tears streaming down her frightened face, but Tom hurried through the living room door behind his Dad. Shocked into action, Danny herded Mum and Abi into the room.

Painful in its brilliance and intensity, a light rushed in with a blue-whiteness that hurt their eyes. It seemed to light the house from within, forcing its way in, creeping through every crack, slanting under the door of each room like the beams of a powerful searchlight as it probed the very structure of the building. It pierced the keyhole of the front door, a brilliant bar of pure light cutting its way into the darkness. Slicing through the small Georgian panes of glass, the curtains covering the windows billowed inwards like the sails of an old schooner under the pressure of the beam. Its presence was so powerful it could be physically felt and still the droning vibration increased, descending heavily from above.

The light continued, its beams throwing contrasted bars of deep shadow into the brightness. Alternate patterns of light and dark moved across the walls and floor, playing games with the furniture, until at last they slowed and were still.

Shielding their eyes against the pain of the light, Tom and Abi held each other for support as the house rocked around them. Shouting to her, Tom asked if she was okay, but he was unable to hear his own voice.

Time seemed to stretch, each second like a minute, each minute like an hour and still the noise intensified. Furniture bounced and scraped where it stood, shifting position as the floor resonated with the vibration beneath. The whole building was in motion and it was as if everything were alive, the pulsing drone deep within them all, shaking everyone to the bone.

Nothing could have prepared them for the silence which followed, piercing their eardrums with the force of a thousand needles. It was a sheer force which caused pain so intense that everyone doubled over, their hands clasped to their ears as their senses reeled.

The stillness felt unnatural. It was as if it had no reason to be there, yet the pressure of the light continued. It pressed against their chests like an ever tightening band making it difficult to breathe. Abi began to cough, the dust clogging her throat as she gasped for breath and sank to the floor. She buried her face deep between her arms, her hands still covering her ears against the loudness of the silence.

Dazed by the assault of light and sudden silence, Abi cried out in great sobs. Her whole body shook, her mind tortured by the experiences which pummelled away at her.

Tom sat down and put his arm around her shoulders, pulling her close.

'Hey, come on,' he said soothingly although his voice betrayed him. It trembled and he was on the verge of tears but fought them back. 'Come on.' He pulled his sister closer but she didn't hear his words as her ears were still recoiling from the sudden silence. She sensed he had said something and raised her head slightly to look at her brother. As she looked into his eyes she saw his terror, his pain, and dissolved into tears once more.

Dust swirled around the room, the currents energised into some kind of wild dance by the vibration and power, but as they squinted against the brightness the dust seemed to slow. Everything remained lit like a ghostly shroud for long seconds until the blinding beams were disturbed. Something blocked the light, preventing it from shining under the front door and new shadows were cast across the flagstones of the hallway. Whatever was outside was joined by others. They shuffled on the stone doorstep and with a creak, the handle turned.

As the door clicked open, the full brightness of the immense light poured through. Instinctively shielding their eyes, they were drawn to look, both hands attempting unsuccessfully to shield the glare...and they saw an unbelieveable vision.

Three small, child-sized figures stood silhouetted against the glare, their bulbous heads and slender, grossly out of proportion fingers casting long shadows into the house. As the figures shuffled quickly and awkwardly down the hallway, panic set in.

The living room door suddenly slammed shut. Dad was shouting at Danny to help him pull the sofa against it, barricading themselves in. They quickly dragged the chairs and piled them on top of the sofa until the doorway was totally blocked.

Shaking in its frame, the door began to rattle violently and the makeshift barrier began to move, sliding across the stone floor. Light poured in through the widening gap.

Fighting their fear Dad and Danny pushed hard against the barricade. The door closed tightly with an audible click but continued to rattle as light spilled through any gap it could find in the frame. Three sets of feet shuffled about in the hallway beyond, their presence blocking the bar of light which beamed under the door, causing long shadows to stretch out across the living room.

A tapping sound drew their attention and for long seconds nobody dared move. The sound was repeated followed by the tinkle of breaking glass.

Rage suddenly kicked in. Mum took a step towards the billowing curtains, her hands balled into fists, her shoulders set hard with determination.

'Don't,' shouted Dad, but she continued.

'I've got to see,' she said, a new found strength suddenly exerting itself. 'This is *my* house and they're *not* doing this to me! I need to know what's out there!' She raised her hands to the curtains, her mind whirling. A thought hit her and she paused for the briefest of seconds. *Why are the curtains blowing? The windows aren't open, I closed them before we went to bed.*

Light shone around the edges of the curtains. Distorted shapes and strange shadows fluttered from behind as they flapped. Finger-like protuberances and thin, almost stick-like limbs flashed briefly into view and then disappeared.

The tapping continued.

Steeling herself, she took hold of the curtains. *How dare they do this to me?* she thought. *My family? My home?* Gripping the curtains she looked back at her husband, her children, and saw their pain. For their sake she needed to see what was going on and nothing was going to change her mind.

With a final deep breath she flung open the curtains.

Nothing could have prepared her for the vision beyond.

CHAPTER 15

Blackness. Deeper and darker than any an artist could paint. Almost invisible, soaking up all ambient light, it made the night sky appear as if the stars had been cut away. Dropping from the sky, the triangular shape hung over a single building. It rotated slowly as it homed in on a solitary signal, a droning hum emanating from somewhere deep inside.

Three lights burst into brightness, one at each corner, their beams narrow, straight and blinding. As the craft spun, they played slowly over the roof top and garden casting distorted patterns as if the heavens were playing games with starlight.

Banks of smaller lights burst into life all over the underside, illuminating everything beneath with such power that to an observer the scene might look like an over exposed photograph. Trees in the garden shone with branches and leaves of reflected silver and the house itself shone radiated with a spiritual light. Changing from white to blue-white and back again the piercing beams speared downwards but somehow remained within the shadow of the triangle, even though the shafts of brilliance would undoubtedly be seen for many miles around.

The surrounding air vibrated and the Old Vicarage became slightly distorted as the craft rotated. Figures appeared, moving with quick, almost nervous movements and within seconds had disappeared inside the building. Others approached the French windows, panes of glass breaking under their long, probing fingers.

The curtains covering the windows billowed, filled with the intense power of light and energy swirling from above.

And then, suddenly, they were parted.

A figure stood there, eyes almost shut against the glare. It shielded its eyes against the overwhelming brightness but saw enough to know that the figures outside were not human.

CHAPTER 16

Mum backed away from the window so quickly that she tripped. Sprawled on her back, her eyes never left the silhouettes. She sat up quickly and scrambled backwards, away from the windows in case they should try to touch her. The unblinking black eyes seemed to pierce her soul.

A whispered, almost infant-like voice filled her head: *You have nothing to fear. We will not harm you.* An overwhelming sense of calm followed, descending through her whole body like a warm wave.

'What is it? What's out there?' Dad left the sofa and picked Mum up. She stood listening for something only she could hear, the feeling of calm continuing, but her instinctive reaction to the vision at the window began to creep in again. She felt her nerves jangle with alarm. She quickly stepped behind her husband, using him as a shield as logic took over.

'No, no, they aren't real...they aren't real,' she mumbled to herself, not taking her eyes from the curtains. 'They can't be!' Her hands covered her face but she stared across the room through open fingers. 'What do they want? What do they want?' Her voice was filled with panic. The door began to rattle again, banging loudly in its frame, before suddenly falling silent. Mum screamed and Dad held her, holding her shaking body for a few seconds before stepping towards the windows. But as he prepared himself for what lay beyond, darkness fell. It covered the entire house like a heavy blanket.

For precious seconds no one could see anything; the light had been so blindingly intense that the sudden darkness was impenetrable and left behind a disorientation which sent the senses reeling.

The heavy drone picked up again from outside, but this time there was no vibration: this time it simply built in intensity until it filled the room. In that instant, Dad knew he had to have some understanding of what he had just experienced, and this was his final chance. Reaching forward, fumbling in the darkness, he found the key still in the lock. The doors swung inwards on a strong breeze from outside and before he knew it, he was standing on the soft grass of the back garden. He didn't notice the broken glass was missing from beneath his feet.

With his eyes and ears still recovering from the assault he didn't expect to see or hear anything, but was mistaken. A bright light, fuzzy in his distorted vision, hovered above him as his eyes turned upwards to look.

His home was dwarfed by the shape overhead: an immense black triangle, its edges hard against the starlit sky as it slowly rotated, each corner illuminated by white lights.

Dazed and disorientated, Danny shuffled out of the room. Tom followed but Abi hung back in the doorway.

The shape began to rise. Slowly and majestically it drifted towards the hillside, the stars blocked from view as it rotated. Even at height its sheer size dwarfed the earthly buildings below.

A lazy ball of light drifted into view from the far side of the house like an ember cast from a summer bonfire. With a sudden burst of speed it sped towards the receding ship like a dog obediently following its master's footsteps, until it shrunk to a glowing pinpoint in the distance.

The lights remained diamond bright in the darkness. Swiftly they reached the distant hilltops where they hung, piercing the heavens – a new constellation in the night sky. For minutes they remained motionless, until their formation smoothly changed. Stretching out, they formed a twinkling line above Urra Moor.

A roar suddenly split the night wide open. Roof tiles and windows rattled with its power as two black shapes thundered overhead, lights winking brightly across their bellies. Three more skimmed the treetops to their left and a sixth to their right. Within seconds they too were pinpoints in the night sky.

Converging quickly on the distant hills they rushed forward with all speed, but it wasn't enough. With a velocity that was frightening, the distant lights streaked upwards and outwards across the face of the sky. They fanned out leaving bright streaks in the darkness which the eye retained for seconds after the lights had diminished, like some sort of cosmic afterglow from the ultimate firework. The navigation lights of the RAF fighters curved upwards to follow them and rose high into the sky as they gave chase, but within seconds their targets had disappeared from sight. Radar screens within the fighters' cockpits showed no return and the pilots levelled off. With nothing to see and nothing to follow they could only turn for home.

Dad sat down heavily. He stared at the distant hilltops while the immensity of events sunk in. Finally he turned to Danny. 'What was that all about?' he asked. 'What did they want?'

Danny looked at Abi standing in the doorway of the

living room. Tom had stepped forward to watch the display and now stood beside his Dad.

'Me,' said Danny. 'They wanted me.'

'You? Why? Why do they want you?'

'I've got something they want, something that belongs to them.'

'What?'

Danny tapped his head with his index finger. 'Knowledge.' He looked troubled, as if revealing what he knew would bring more down on them. 'I know their secret,' he said, and after a pause added, 'I know why they're here.'

Mum cleared her throat but didn't speak. Danny continued. 'I know everything: who they are, where they're from, and most importantly…' his voice dropped, '…what they want with us.' He looked frightened again. 'It's been a secret for a very long time.'

Dumbfounded, Dad opened his mouth to speak but Mum spoke for him. 'I think you've got some explaining to do,' she said. She looked him sternly in the eye, then stepped back into the room.

CHAPTER 17

The room was in total disarray and so were Dad's thoughts. He stood, dazedly looking for the door, and remembered it was behind the sofa. With an effort of will he stepped back into his own world.

Moving nervously into the hallway, the dry smell of dust still lingered in the air. Ornaments lay scattered across the stone flags of the hallway, their broken pieces like some kind of obscene confetti.

Dad opened the kitchen door slowly, not sure what he would find on the other side. Mum followed him through and began picking up broken crockery and smashed photograph frames from the floor. The idea of leaving the stone floor uncovered had seemed like a good idea when they moved in because it had been such a beautiful feature, but it had turned into an instrument of destruction. The evidence lay scattered around them.

Tom and Abi looked around nervously before sitting down. Mum picked up the old steam kettle from the floor. It had always been a bit battered but had a few more dents now. Mum had bought it from a junk shop shortly after moving in, saying it fit the atmosphere of the kitchen more than an electric kettle and made a better cup of tea. She placed it gently back on the range and began picking up tea bags which were strewn across the floor.

Dad opened a locked cupboard and pulled out a bottle of something coppery-brown. 'Anyone?' he asked, picking up a couple of unbroken mugs from the unit top where they had somehow escaped the destruction.

'Good idea.' The two men sat down and Dad shook the bottle as a way of asking Mum if she wanted to join them. She picked up a plastic beaker and slumped into a seat.

'Would you two like a drink of something?' Mum turned to Tom and Abi. Still stunned from the events of the past hour they mumbled something, and Tom poured a drink of juice for Abi and himself. The adults sat sipping brandy for a few minutes and then Mum climbed to her feet. 'Come on,' she said, 'let's put everything straight.' Tom could tell by her actions she was very agitated.

As Mum and Dad worked their way around the kitchen, Tom and Abi followed closely. When the tidying continued upstairs they followed quickly, not wanting to be left alone downstairs.

Conversation was short, distracted, and Abi said nothing. She seemed as if she were elsewhere, her thoughts not in tune with those of the people around her.

Mum opened the landing cupboard and picked up a dustpan and brush, ready to sweep up the bigger pieces of glass from the floor in the spare room while Dad brought the vacuum cleaner, but when they entered the room they found the carpet was spotlessly clean and the window unbroken. Mum and Dad looked at each other, unable to believe what they were seeing. 'This is weird,' muttered Dad. 'What on earth happened?'

Danny's feet on the staircase sounded hurried. He stopped in the doorway, his voice full of disbelief at what he had found downstairs. 'Pete. The doors. I could have sworn the glass was broken, but now...' He stepped into the room where he had spent the night, saw the window intact, the carpet clear of glass, and stopped mid sentence. He looked around, not knowing what to say as Dad stepped towards the door, muttering to himself as he pushed past his friend. His words were full of disbelief.

'I need another drink.'

'What time is it?' Mum asked as she sat cradling her drink.

Dad glanced at the clock behind her head. 'Quarter past four.' He turned to the children. 'Would you two like to go back to bed?' he asked, knowing the reply he would get before the words had even left his mouth. Tom and Abi just shook their heads, their eyes betraying their emotions.

'Why don't you lie down on the living room sofa?' asked Mum. 'We'll leave the door open and you can see and hear us. We're not going anywhere, I promise.'

Tom thought for a moment and then stood up. Abi watched him, then slowly climbed to her feet.

In the living room Mum switched on a table lamp and settled Tom and Abi down. She sat with them for a while and they talked quietly, Abi huddling close until she drifted into sleep. Tom smiled at Mum and sat back. He put his feet up beside her and placed his hand tenderly on his sister's leg. *I'll take care of her. I'm her big brother*, the gesture said.

By the time Mum returned to the kitchen, the two men were talking in forced whispers.

'...people would never believe us, but surely someone *must* have seen or heard something. Something like tonight can't go unnoticed.'

Danny looked at Dad and pursed his lips. Dad went on. 'You know the stigma that's attached to these things. If I hadn't experienced it myself I wouldn't have believed it, but if we tell anyone about it they'll think we've gone crazy.' He sat back and took another gulp of his drink.

'That's always been the problem; nobody believes you. I know that better than anybody.' Danny sounded hurt, his voice emotional.

'Look Danny, I know I had a hard time believing you before. At the time I was sceptical, but after tonight, after what I've seen...' Dad paused and his voice dropped. 'I'm sorry about before, I really am.' The two men looked at each other and Dad raised the bottle, asking a silent question with raised eyebrows. Danny nodded and pushed his mug forward.

'You mean this has happened before?' asked Mum, her face a mask of tension and unease as she sat down.

Danny nodded. He looked guarded. 'I can't be specific about what happened because I don't recall too much about it,' he said, 'but I do remember bright lights and a feeling of floating. And I remember the eyes.' He glanced into his drink, swirling the liquid around for a few seconds before looking up.

'He shared it with me,' said Dad, 'but somehow it got out.' His voice sounded like an admission.

'Did you...?' Mum looked shocked at Dad's indiscretion, but he shook his head firmly, his face carrying an indignant look.

'No! Definitely not!' he said, 'but that was when we fell out. I didn't believe Danny and he thought I'd told others, which I hadn't. When the story got around I made a choice, a wrong choice as it happens. I didn't stick by my friend. I thought that siding with Danny would harm my street credibility – that I wouldn't look cool and so I walked away.' Dad looked Mum straight in the eye. 'You know how it is when you're that age. It's difficult.' He gave a sheepish smile.

'I was obsessed with UFOs all through my youth,' said Danny. 'I read and watched everything I could: books; magazines; all kinds of movies and TV shows. But even though I eventually managed to put it behind me, it was still there, lurking in the shadows waiting to come out again.'

The pause that followed was uncomfortable but eventually Mum spoke. 'I've heard some things about UFOs,' she said, 'but I haven't given them much thought. They haven't really interested me.' Mum shifted in her seat before continuing, as if she couldn't bring herself to ask the next question. 'So those things tonight...?'

'Greys. They're known as Greys.' Danny said it quietly as if speaking the words aloud would bring them back.

'Greys?'

'That's what they are. Their bodies are grey, small, almost childlike in appearance but with large heads and big eyes. Big black eyes.'

'And the light?'

'I don't know why, but they seem to mask themselves with it.'

'And that was their ship?'

Danny nodded. 'Witnesses speak of mysterious shapes – usually discs – but more recently black triangles. For years people thought they were secret military aircraft, but they move so much faster than anything we have.' He held up his hands in exasperation before continuing. 'You saw for yourself.'

Mum sat thoughtfully, focused on her inner-self before looking up with a puzzled expression on her face. 'I remember hearing about something that had crashed somewhere abroad. Ros…something?'

Dad and Danny exchanged a knowing look. 'Roswell,' said Danny. 'You're talking about Roswell.'

'That's it,' said Mum clicking her fingers, stray memories starting to fit together. 'Didn't they find alien bodies or something?'

'Yeah. The story goes that in 1947, a UFO crashed in the desert outside Roswell. The military recovered four bodies.' He looked at Dad then carried on. 'They were taken to Roswell Air Force base along with the wreckage of the ship, but the US Government say it never happened. They say it was a weather balloon that came down, even though people who worked on the recovery have since broken silence and told what they know.'

'And they still deny it happened?' asked Mum incredulously.

Both men nodded slowly.

'Has anything else like that happened? Over here, for example?'

'Oh, yes,' said Danny, his tone enforcing his belief. 'There are some quite famous encounters, but not always involving crashed spaceships. Rendlesham Forest is well-documented: something was supposed to have landed in the forest outside an American air base. Twice, and on consecutive nights.'

'So why haven't we heard about these...visits?'

'They're either denied or explained away,' said Danny, 'but the truth has started to come out in recent years.' He paused, then added, 'Don't you ever watch *Discovery Channel?*'

Mum laughed but was startled all the same. 'So if it's the truth, who denies it? Why deny it?'

'The powers-that-be,' said Dad. 'The Government.' Danny nodded slowly, thoughtfully.

Mum paused, stunned to silence. 'The Government?' she asked, but then waved her hand, dismissing the thought. 'Never mind,' she said, 'carry on.'

'Then there was a mass sighting of UFOs in Belgium a few years back. I'm not talking of one or two sightings, either. I'm talking about over two thousand lights, ships, whatever you want to call them. They were reported to be flying in a triangular formation as if attached to the underside of some enormous craft.'

Dad leaned forward, his mug now empty and put to one side. 'And it goes back further than that. In the 1930s and '40s, Spitfire pilots and bombers crews reported strange craft dodging around them, teasing them. Some were like fairy lights but others resembled the modern designs we've come to see in the media.'

'They nicknamed them Foo Fighters,' added Danny, 'but they've been visiting here as long ago as mediaeval times, perhaps even longer. Throughout history strange lights and inexplicable phenomena in the sky were treated as omens: some good; some bad. They believed they were witnessing angels or dragons in the sky. It must have been terrifying.'

Dad stood up, placed his mug in the sink and returned the half empty bottle to the cupboard. He locked the door quietly and turned to face the others. 'And there have been other sightings, other encounters all over the world. Not just here and in America, but in France, Russia, Brazil – almost every country has reported sightings, and they keep on happening.'

Mum sat back and folded her arms, pondering what she had heard, then turned to Danny and asked the question that the whole conversation had been leading to. 'And you know why they're here?'

Danny nodded slowly. He seemed pensive, thoughtful.

'What do you mean, you know?' asked Mum. 'Do you *really* know why they're here, or are you just guessing?'

Danny paused, his face etched with tension. He shuffled in his seat. 'I know,' he said. 'I really know.' He glanced between Mum and Dad before speaking again. When he did, he spoke slowly as if every word counted.

'They have a secret,' he said, leaning forward. 'I know what it is, and they don't like it.'

CHAPTER 18

Tom sat on the sofa; Abi dozed beside him. She'd stirred twice in the past few minutes and shifted position as she mumbled to herself, but Tom knew she wasn't fully asleep. Nevertheless, he was glad she had managed to rest.

He tried to listen to the adults talking, but could only make out occasional words. The tone of the conversation was not altogether good, as it had been when he'd brought his school report home at the end of the summer term.

Mum and Dad had been more concerned than angry, asking him why he wasn't working to his best. They'd put it down to him being a little unsettled in a new school, having to make new friends and the fact that village life wasn't quite what Tom had expected. They'd worked hard trying to help him fit in and he had eventually made stronger friendships in the latter part of the year.

Tom yawned and found himself drifting towards sleep. His legs jolted him awake several times, the way they do when your mind is in a deep sleep but your body hasn't quite relaxed yet, and tried to focus on the conversation coming from the kitchen.

In his half awake, half asleep state he heard things he didn't really understand: *Greys... triangles... Roswell... Rendlesham...* and then something he had heard before.

Foo Fighters.

As he drifted down into the warm softness of slumber his brain mulled the words over...*Dad likes the Foo Fighters*, it thought. *They're an American rock band. Why are they talking about music?*

The adults sat looking at each other in silence, the implications of Danny's words too great to comprehend.

'So what are you going to do?' asked Dad

Danny held his head in his hands and let out a long, slow breath. 'I don't know,' he said at last, then rubbed his eyes and looked up at the ceiling, his hands clasped behind his head and his arms jutting out like a pair of wings.

'If they know you've got this knowledge...and they do...they're going to take it back somehow, whether you want them to or not,' said Dad. 'You know that, don't you? They tried tonight and they're going to try again. You don't really have any say in the matter.'

'I know, I know, I know,' groaned Danny, leaning heavily on the table. 'It's just that I don't want to go back up there. I can't face going through it all again.'

'Go through what?' asked Mum.

Danny dropped his eyes until they met Mum's. 'I ... I can't tell you that. I can't, so please, please, don't ask me any more, okay? It's for your own good.'

'Why? What's so secretive?'

Danny fixed Mum with an intense stare. 'If I tell you, they'll know. Believe me. Then they'll be after you as well. Are you ready for that? Are you really ready, 'cos if I tell you, then you'll become part of this as well.' Danny looked at Dad and then back to Mum again.

'They'll want you and I'm not prepared to put you through that. I think I've brought enough trouble to your door, don't you?'

The atmosphere chilled suddenly. Mum shivered again, not for the first time that night, and wrapped her robe a little more tightly around herself.

The kitchen fell silent and in the distance a cockerel crowed. They hadn't noticed that daylight had crept in through the kitchen window and the sky had brightened towards sunrise while they talked.

Mum stood up and went to the door. Turning the key, she stepped through into the growing light of dawn and somehow felt more secure, as if the events of the night before had never happened. This was her world and nothing was ever going to spoil it for her. Nothing.

Dad slipped his arm gently around her waist and together they stepped onto the lawn. A few birds had begun their daily wake-up ritual, chirping and trilling with an enthusiasm for life, as if for the first time. The chorus was soon picked up by others and before long the air was filled with birdsong. It was a symphony of beauty, clear in the still morning air.

'Listen to that,' said Dad quietly. 'Wonderful.'

Mum turned her face up to the sky, a slight coolness of night air still lingering, and closed her eyes. Breathing deeply she tasted the sweet scent of honeysuckle and for a few moments felt herself relax totally. The tension in her neck and shoulders trickled away like water, and her whole body sagged. She walked over to the wooden bench and eased herself onto it, feeling exhausted all at once.

Dad watched her. 'You okay?' he asked.

She folded her arms around herself. 'Mm-hm,' she said and smiled. Dad didn't believe the smile but decided not to challenge it. How could she be alright after what they had just been through?

Dad walked over to inspect the glass doors he had opened to watch the ship take off. The windows were intact. There were no signs of any damage, not even footprints or scorch marks on the grass. He'd expected to find something. He looked around, puzzled.

Danny joined him and together they stood looking up at the distant hills. Urra Moor appeared out of the gloom. The light ship had hovered there as if it were baiting the fighters until it had split into four and vanished. Dad still couldn't quite believe what he had seen.

Neither man spoke but Danny finally broke the silence with the decision that both he and Dad knew had to be made. 'All you have to do is get me close to the hills, to where I need to be,' he said quietly. 'I'll do the rest. I'll give them back what they want, then this will all go away.'

'Us,' said Dad without looking at Danny. 'You mean us.'

He turned to look at his friend. 'No. This isn't about you. You don't need to get any more involved than you already are. You stay h…'

'I'm coming with you,' said Dad. He turned to face Danny and grabbed him by the shoulders. 'I owe it to you and I owe it us. It's the thing I should have done all those years ago.'

Danny looked into his friend's eyes and saw determination lingering there. 'Do you have any idea of what's involved?' he asked, his face betraying the hardships to come.

'No, but together we'll get through it. We always managed to wriggle our way through everything else, didn't we?' Dad laughed and Danny cracked a grin. It was the same familiar grin from all those years ago.

'Yeah, we did. We did.'

Dad dropped his hands. 'We've always taught the kids that their friends are important, that you don't let them down. How can I step back from that? If I did I'd be making a mockery of the way we've brought up our family.' He paused, thinking for a moment. 'How would I be able to look my children in the face? The morals we've worked so hard to teach them wouldn't be worth much then, would they?'

Danny nodded. 'I see what you mean.'

CHAPTER 19

Mum had taken Tom and Abi up to bed leaving both men to ponder their thoughts together in the garden's early morning stillness.

Dad broke the silence. 'Well?' His tone was direct.

Danny knew what his friend was asking and opened his mouth several times to speak. Finally he found his voice. 'It's …awesome. Mind-blowing. You have no idea.' He shook his head, unable to comprehend the implications of the knowledge he possessed.

Stepping into the kitchen, Danny pulled a chair from

under the table and sat down heavily. Dad rummaged around in a kitchen drawer looking for something, then turned to face Danny.

Leaning forward Danny rested his elbows on his knees and picked at his nails. He was agitated but after a few tense moments started to speak.

'This whole thing...it's like nothing you've ever thought about or heard before,' he said. He stood up and walked over to the sink, filled a glass with water and took a deep swallow. Leaning on the edge of the sink with his shoulders hunched and his back to Dad he continued. 'It's going to blow the lid off so many ideas, so many theories and religious beliefs – beliefs about the world and where we came from.'

He turned around and looked at Dad, his expression startled and frightened. 'It's going to blow them wide open and it's going to change everything. Absolutely everything.'

CHAPTER 20

Tom awoke to the sound of breakfast pots clattering and the smell of bacon. He closed his eyes, trying to drift back into sleep, but his mind was awash with images from the evening before.

His short sleep had been disturbed by shapes which drifted through his mind, floating into and over each other like some giant kaleidoscope. As he rested, his pillow soft and familiar beneath his head, he tried to remember the names he had heard in the last seconds before sleep had claimed him. Somehow he knew they were important.

'Foo Fighters,' he said to himself. 'Yeah, that was it. Foo Fighters.' He furrowed his brow as he tried to remember the other names. 'Roz...yeah, Roz something.' But the final name? He couldn't pull it from his brain no matter how hard he tried. He knew it began with R.

Ren... Ren... but couldn't get any further than that. He pursed his lips in frustration.

Mum opened his door quietly and the delicious smell of warm bacon wafted in with her. 'Here you are,' she said, 'I thought you might be awake.'

She sat down next to him, smiled and smoothed his hair as he sat up. 'Mum, about last night...'

'I think we should try our best to forget all about that,' she said tensely. 'Forget about it. It's for the best. It really is.'

She obviously didn't want to talk about it and it all seemed dream-like now in the light of day. He took the bacon sandwich from her and started eating, brown sauce dribbling between his fingers. He licked it off with a slurp and Mum laughed. She stood up and watched him as he took another bite, but when she spoke her words were nervous. 'I need you to go to Mary's today. Both of you, okay?'

'Where are you going?' asked Tom, his mouth half full of breakfast. He watched her and immediately saw the tight way in which she held herself. *She looks nervous,* thought Tom, but didn't enquire further. Somehow he knew he shouldn't.

'Can you be ready by 9 ?'

Tom glanced at the clock beside his bed and nodded.

Mum smiled and stepped towards the door. She paused slightly as she closed it behind her and then was gone.

Tom sat idly chewing his breakfast, thinking things over when a thought hit him. He stopped mid swallow. If he went to Mary's she might let him visit the library by himself. It was only a few minutes away.

He jumped out of bed, grabbed a scrap of paper from the bin, and hurriedly scribbled two words:

roz   ren

Folding the paper, he pushed it into the pocket of his jeans, stuffed the remains of the sandwich into his mouth and dashed towards the bathroom.

As he passed the landing window he glanced outside, and in a heartbeat the world around him was still. A dark, shrouded figure stood on the far side of the road against the dry stone wall. Everything about it was unusual, from its coal-black suit and tie set against a shirt so crystal white that it shone as if fluorescent, to its wide-brimmed hat which cast a shadow over the face beneath. It was a shadow so deep it was impossible to see the face below.

The world seemed to twist around itself, fading away as the dark figure loomed forward into focus, its darkness reaching out to Tom. He saw the figure raise its hand and his mind flashed.

You will understand.

The words flooded his mind and he was unsure whether he heard them or felt them. Tom shuddered and blinked. When he looked again the figure was gone.

* * *

The fresh light of summer morning accompanied the car as it pulled away from the kerb. The hedgerows and stone walls sped past as Tom watched for the figure he had seen only fifteen minutes before. The village soon changed to open countryside and his thoughts drifted as the car turned out of the village and followed the signs for Little Ayton. His mind was preoccupied with earlier events and it took a while for him to notice that nobody had spoken since leaving home. He could feel the tension as taut as a guitar string amongst the adults and wished someone would say something to break the ice. Finally, Mum and Dad struck up a conversation and the atmosphere seemed to ease a little.

Tom watched his Dad carefully. He noticed his right hand absently check his jacket pocket several times, at one point nervous fingers undoing the zip and fidgeting around inside. Tom saw a brief flash of yellow-orange paper but nothing more.

The car wound its way along narrow roads before it

slowed to cross a low iron bridge at Grange Farm. There the beck ran alongside the road towards Great Ayton, shadowing them as they went. Red pan-tiles and grey slate rooftops drifted into view, carefully manicured flowerbeds and window boxes full of nasturtiums, pansies and marigolds shedding colour in every direction.

It was only 9:15 and Great Ayton was just starting to come to life. The high street opposite the village green was quiet so Mum pulled off the main road and parked in front of the pub, The Royal Oak. A tense silence hung in the car for a few seconds after the engine died and Dad sat, his lips pursed in thought, before finally speaking. When he did, Tom felt it like a bolt of electricity and jumped.

'Right, then,' he said, 'we'll only be a few minutes. Meet you back here?'

Mum nodded. 'I'll nip over to Mary's with Tom and Abi. I shouldn't be long, but if I'm not back just wait for me.'

Dad turned around to face Tom and Abi. 'You two be good today, okay? I'll see you tonight.'

Abi spoke for the first time since leaving home, her question direct and the one Dad had been dreading most of all. 'Where are you going?'

Dad looked uncomfortable but quickly recovered himself, his nervous expression replaced by a big smile for his daughter's benefit. 'Danny and I have decided to go on a walk together. We haven't done that for years, have we?' He twisted in his seat and looked at Danny again, raising his eyebrows.

Danny nodded. 'Mm. That's right. Yes.' His reply was forced, rehearsed, and not very convincing.

Tom piped up. 'This is to do with last night, isn't it

Dad?'

'No, no, no.' He couldn't hide his surprise at the intensity of the question. 'Of course not. We've just decided to catch up on a bit of walking, for old times' sake.'

Tom didn't believe a word but thought it best not to ask any more.

Standing outside the car in a small family group like any other, Dad hugged his children tightly, the kind of hug he gave if he wasn't going to see them for a while.

'Now you be good and I'll see you tonight,' he repeated. He put his hand on Tom's shoulder and Tom turned his back slightly towards Abi so that she wouldn't see his lips. 'Be careful, Dad,' he mouthed.

Father and son looked at each other in a way only they understood and Dad nodded, then he squeezed his son's shoulder and turned away.

CHAPTER 21

As Mary opened the door, Abi flung her arms tightly around her Mum's waist. 'Mum, I want to come with you.' She looked up into her mother's eyes, her expression pleading and frightened. 'Please, Mum.'

'Hey, now. What's all this?' Mum cast an apologetic look at Mary as she squatted down beside her daughter.

Mary smiled. 'Why don't you come in and talk about it? Come on, we'll all have a drink and a biscuit. Tea, anybody?'

Tom stepped quickly into the room, its high ceiling and old oak beams towering above him. The flat had originally been one of the rooms on the top floor of the Old Friends' School, and Tom liked it here.

Mum and Abi sat down while Tom and Mary made their way into the kitchen. 'She's a bit upset,' whispered Tom when they were out of earshot. He didn't elaborate further. How could he? What would he say? *Well, you see, this big spaceship came and landed right on top of our house last night…*

Mary knew it wouldn't be anything personal. 'We'll let them talk. Come and help me make the tea.'

As Mary busied herself with the kettle, Tom picked up the biscuit tin and tucked it under his arm. She always kept it well-stocked and Tom smiled as he prized the lid off. *Mmm*, he thought. *Chocolate. My favourite!*

'What's this all about?' asked Mum. Abi sat with her hands entwined around her Mum's arm and pulled herself close. When she didn't speak, Mum coaxed her a little more. 'Come on, Abi. If there's something wrong then I need to know.' She knew full well what was eating away at Abi's emotions.

Abi raised her head, and, when she spoke, her voice was thin and timid. 'I'm frightened.'

Mum cupped Abi's face with her free hand. 'Frightened of what?' She felt her own emotions surface as the events of the early hours played across her daughter's face. 'What are you frightened of, Abi?'

'Please don't leave me here. I want to go with you today.'

Mum untangled herself from Abi's grip and twisted herself round so they were sat face to face. 'Abi, last night's over. It won't happen again.'

'But it might.'

'Trust me. It's over.'

'But why can't I stay with you? Why do I have to stay here?'

Mum smiled. 'You know Mary is my best friend and you know you're always welcome here. Please, stay here, just for today while your Dad and I sort a few things out. We'll be back for you before you know it.' Mum smiled again. 'I promise.'

Abi stated to cry. 'But I want to come with you. Please, Mum. Don't leave me here.' She looked at her Mum, tears spilling from her eyes, and Mum knew she couldn't leave Abi in such a state. The sight of her sobbing so desperately pulled at Mum's heart and she sat for a moment, the argument for Tom and Abi staying with Mary running over and over in her mind. It seemed more sensible for them to be away from home until the situation with Danny had passed, but she supposed she could take them with her. It wasn't as if she were going anywhere dangerous, and they could all be there to pick up Dad as arranged.

Mum made up her mind. 'Tom, can you come here a moment, please?'

Tom stepped into the living room, biscuit crumbs dusting the corners of his mouth as he crunched his way through his third chocolate biscuit in as many minutes.

'Listen, Tom. Abi really wants to come with me today.'

Tom shook his head and mumbled a reply, crumbs dropping onto the carpet as he spoke. He crunched a little more, then swallowed, managing to speak around the half-eaten biscuit. 'I want to stay here.' His thoughts were instantly on his plan, and he didn't want it spoiled.

'Are you sure? We can have a nice day out, just the

three of us…'

Tom nodded. 'I'm sure.' *If Abi goes with Mum, I won't have her hanging around me all day. I'll be able to do what I want*, he thought. *Great!*

Mum thought for a moment. 'I feel terrible now, planning to leave you here without really asking what you wanted to do. If I'd known it was such a big issue, I wouldn't have brought you here.'

'Mum, it's fine.' Tom was desperate that Mum leave him. His plan depended on it.

'Are you sure you don't mind?'

Tom shook his head. He didn't mind at all.

As the car pulled away from its space outside the pub, Tom sat talking to Mary over a glass of juice. Ten minutes later he was on his way down two flights of stairs, jogging towards the high street.

He'd never been eager to get to the library before, but today he was on a mission. He ran over the village green and stopped at the curb by the statue of Captain Cook to let a delivery van and a few cars pass. As he waited he read the inscription:

JAMES COOK
who lived in Great Ayton
between 1736 and 1745
Later became Captain James Cook
R.N.F.R.S
Famous Navigator

Tom had studied Captain Cook in a project at school

just before the summer holidays. It had interested him more than any other subject he had studied all year, but that had been about the limit of his interest and he had found the rest of school rather boring. His report had said much the same thing.

As he stood looking at the statue he wondered what strange and exciting things Cook must have encountered on his travels. He remembered that Cook had discovered Australia, New Zealand and Easter Island, but what else had he found? Pirate treasure? Hidden cities of gold? The thought of it was exciting.

There was something about Cook's life which appealed to Tom; taking off into the unknown, discovering new places full of wonder. It all had some kind of a draw to it. *I wonder what he'd have made of these strange happenings,* Tom thought as a car pulled out of a parking space in front of him. *I wonder.*

The road soon cleared and Tom stepped out, knowing Mary would be watching him from the living room window. He turned and gave her a little wave as he reached the 'phone box. She returned it before disappearing into the shadows and Tom walked quickly past a row of square-fronted shops, following the path as it dipped gently away to the right.

A raised footpath rose away from the road as it meandered past a café and *Suggit's* ice cream shop. Tom dipped a hand into the pocket of his jeans and fingered the money there, thinking seriously about stopping but decided against it. He quickened his pace again, weaving between the few early shoppers before finally slowing to look at the old sandstone building in front of him. An inscription beside the door told him it had originally been built as a Quaker school in 1843 but turned into a library in 1971. Tom didn't quite know what a Quaker school was, but decided today wasn't the day to find out.

Today he had other things on his mind. He stood looking at the open doorway, took a deep breath and stepped inside.

Are all libraries like this? Tom thought as he stood by the high wooden desk.

Long rows of shelves crammed with books of all sizes seemed to stare at him, their spines promising a world of facts and knowledge, but their smell made his throat gag. He coughed, startled at the loudness of his own noise in the almost silent building, and then covered his mouth with an arm to stifle the noise in case he coughed a second time.

Looking around, he saw a few figures: an old man pouring over his morning paper at startlingly close range and an old lady with a couple of small children focused on the books before them. But Mr Lampard was nowhere to be seen; in fact no one had paid any attention to Tom's entrance. He felt relieved and stepped towards the aim of his morning.

Books. But where to start?

Tom pulled the paper from his back pocket and unfolded it, the sound loud in the stillness. Untidy scribbled handwriting stared back at him, and he stood for a moment thinking. *Spaceships...aliens...roz...ren...what does it all mean? Where do I start?*

He walked slowly forward and quickly scanned the contents of the shelves in front of him, then the next, and the next. His idea had seemed like a good one at the time, but now, faced with all these books, he wasn't so sure any more.

The first tightness of panic began settling itself into his chest and throat, and for an instant he seriously thought about turning to run.

When a heavy hand landed on his shoulder he jumped, a voice from behind startling him. Tom tried to swallow but a dry lump had lodged itself firmly in his throat, and he started to cough.

* * *

Danny hitched his rucksack higher onto his back and tightened the hip strap. They'd stopped for a five minute break, but were eager to keep moving.

Dad had a map in his hand, but neither of them needed it. Both men knew these paths from childhood. The hedges and thick wicker grass were as familiar now as they had always been. *Sure*, thought Dad, *things have changed a bit here and there, but it's essentially the same. A few new fences and hedgerows don't make that much difference.*

The day was already warm and the cloudless sky promised another relentless beating from the sun. A slight wind ghosted its way across the open fields and carried with it the sound of traffic from the Guisborough road, dimming now as it dropped away into the distance, but for the most part the morning was silent. Birds twittering in the hedges and trees were the only real sound. At times, even they fell silent, leaving the crunch and scrape of boots on the well-worn track, and their *whish whish whish* against the grass, when they left the path, as the only sound in the stillness.

Danny became more subdued as they walked, seeming to carry more than the weight of his rucksack. Dad tried talking to him about people and events from their past, their childhood, but by the time they stopped for another break Danny was in a world of his own. He didn't seem to want to talk and walked slightly ahead of Dad. Whenever Dad tried to begin a conversation it seemed to fall on deaf ears and Dad realised Danny needed his own space. He knew when best to leave things to take their own course and dropped back a few paces to let Danny have the solitude he needed.

* * *

Mr Lampard asked the question again, his eyes boring into Tom with the relentlessness of a drill.

'What are you looking for, Sonny?'

Tom realised the voice was directed at him. He opened his mouth to speak, but couldn't find the words. The paper slipped from his fingers and fluttered to the floor with a barely-audible sound. Mr Lampard continued to stare at Tom for a few seconds and then, as slowly as in a dream, he bent and picked up the scrap by its corner. His long fingers held it with reverence, as if it were delicate and would break into a million pieces at the slightest touch.

Tom heard a large intake of breath and realised he'd taken it himself.

'Are you alright?' The voice sounded concerned and Tom noticed Mr Lampard was looking at him more closely.

He stammered a reply and felt the heat of anxiety flood through his body. His throat felt suddenly tight and he gasped again, this time catching his breath.

'Steady now, son.' A big hand gently pushed him backwards into a chair and Tom coughed several times.

When he had finished, he looked nervously up into a careworn face, its skin creased and wrinkled with the deep lines of age, and for the first time Tom saw something else, something he hadn't seen before. The eyes, which had always unnerved him and he had always thought to be black were in fact brown. They were the darkest brown he had ever seen. Merged with the blackness of the pupils, they created a penetrating stare. They were so deep that, for an instant, Tom thought there was nothing there at all. But then he blinked and saw them for what they really were: the dark and watery eyes of an old man.

In an instant Tom realised why he had been so frightened by those eyes in the past. They had reached into his nightmares and plucked unconscious visions with which to terrorise his waking moments, but they were not as he had imagined. Their blackness was unusual, but was simply the product of very dark irises.

At this close distance Tom could see into the eyes and he found something there which surprised him.

Kindness.

The face was framed by a shock of thick white hair which stood up in all directions, as if in rebellion against brush and comb. It gave the face a wild appearance – not unlike that of a mad scientist – but the smile, although slightly crooked, reached upwards towards the eyes and tugged gently at their corners, widening them ever so slightly to create a look of warmth. When Mr Lampard spoke again, his voice was still sharp, but had developed a softer edge which belied the warmth beneath. Tom felt himself begin to relax and a sense of calm flooded over him.

'Aren't you the same fella who passed out in here the

other day?'

Tom smiled sheepishly and managed to croak a reply. 'Yes. Sorry about that.'

'Oh, no need to apologise. Are you feeling okay today? You still don't seem so light on your feet.'

Tom gathered himself together. 'I'm fine, thanks. You just took me by surprise.'

Mr. Lampard watched Tom for a few more seconds and grunted, accepting the explanation before pulling his glasses from his breast pocket. He slipped them on, his eyes suddenly magnified behind them, and with a grunt of satisfaction looked at the slip of paper.

'Now then. What can I help you with, young man?'

CHAPTER 22

The car engine died and Mum sat still for a moment before turning towards Abi. She smiled. 'Are you hungry?'

Abi shook her head, the smile returned, and Mum felt the warmth of their mother-daughter relationship, the warmth they always felt when they were doing things together. *Girlie things*, Tom called them.

'Come on, then,' said Mum as she unclipped her seat belt. Before long they were striding out across the fields in the full heat of a glorious summer day, the sky blue and cloudless and the birds whistling and chirping to each other from the trees.

They talked about this and that, neither mentioning the night before, or their conversation at Mary's, and enjoyed the relaxed atmosphere of the moment. Within ten minutes they were out of sight of the road and were in the middle of open countryside. They saw no one else and liked it that way. A few sheep grazing on the far side of the field kept them company as they walked while the beauty of the day, with its glorious summer colours, enfolded them in a familiar and happy glow.

Ahead stood Roseberry Topping, its green hillside contrasting with the rugged, earthy colours of its sandstone peak as it stood bold against the summer sky. Mum bent to point out some feature to Abi, cheek to cheek with her daughter as she pointed, and Abi nodded. Mum kissed her forehead gently as she stood up and together they continued on as a couple of swallows darted around overhead, disappearing into the trees which now carpeted the horizon on either side.

Crossing into the field beyond, they settled themselves in the shade of a large oak tree, its branches full with the deep-green leaves of summer. Abi began picking daisies and chaining them together while Mum sat and watched. They giggled and talked, resting in the coolness of the shade while the day crept slowly by around them.

Mum closed her eyes and leant back against the solidity of the trunk as somewhere above a thrush burst into song. Its trilling stood out against that of the other birds like a symphony of life and Mum smiled. It sounded so beautiful, so emotional, as if it were singing for a final time, and then stopped – suddenly, abruptly, as if cut off mid-phrase. The silence was so out of place that Mum opened her eyes and listened, her head inclined towards the branches above.

Something seemed wrong, although she couldn't immediately place what it was. It took her a few seconds to comprehend that everything around her had fallen silent. The only sound was her own breathing, loud in the stillness. She climbed to her feet and stepped forward into the sunlight, squinting in its brightness.

'Mum, what's wrong?' Abi followed her Mum and slipped her hand into the comforting warmth of her Mum's, squeezing tightly.

'I don't know.' Mum stood looking around. 'That bird just suddenly...stopped singing. Everything is so quiet. Don't you think that's strange?'

They took a few steps into the open and turned a complete circle. 'This all seems wrong,' Mum said quietly.

They were both looking across the field towards

Roseberry Topping when goose-bumps prickled Mum's arms and neck. Suddenly chilled, the heat seemed to disappear from the sun. Abi felt it too and shivered.

Mum looked down at her daughter and saw she was shaking with the sudden cold. Dropping to her knees, she wrapped her arms around the thin figure and pulled her close. 'Come on, Abi, we're going,' she said as she stood, but a feeling of unease crept in and enveloped her body. She turned towards the path they had followed from the car park but Abi didn't move. 'Abi, come *on*,' she said again and pulled at Abi's shoulder, trying to pull her into motion, but Abi remained immobile.

In the stillness Abi made only the slightest of sounds, but Mum heard it. She knelt by her daughter as Abi spoke again, her whisper a strange sound in the eerie silence. Mum took hold of Abi's face and turned it towards her. 'What did you say?'

Abi's eyes were blank as she continued to murmur words which Mum didn't recognise. They sounded as if they belonged to another language and Mum suddenly felt very scared. Her voice rose in fear until she was almost shouting. 'Abi! Come on. Snap out of it! Please!'

Abi didn't move and Mum started to panic, shaking her daughter by the shoulders. 'What's the matter with you? Oh, God, what's the matter? Abi!' She pulled Abi tightly to her chest, the tears streaming down her face, but she didn't respond. Mum sobbed into her shoulder as Abi continued whispering.

Mum wiped her eyes with shaking hands, and between the tears she saw that everything around her was still: the leaves on the trees which had swayed gently in the summer breeze were motionless. The trees themselves had been frozen mid-movement; their branches held as if in some kind of freeze-frame. The long wicker grass which usually flowed in the breeze like an ocean lay caught in mid flow. Even on the calmest of days, there should be some movement, but, today, at this very moment, there was none.

Absolute stillness covered the world and it was totally silent.

Mum felt her gaze pulled upwards towards the sky. At first she didn't register what she was seeing, and it took a few seconds before her brain began to make sense of it, but then her eyes widened and her throat drained of all moisture.

'Oh, my God,' she said. 'Oh, my God.' Her voice was so dry it came out as a whisper, her throat hurting with the effort, but she didn't seem to notice.

Above her, their wings outstretched in flight, two birds hung in the cloudless sky as if floating on the currents of a warm wind.

But neither bird was moving.

CHAPTER 23

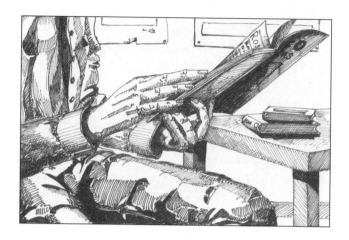

'You haven't got much to go on here,' said Mr Lampard as he looked up from reading the scrap of paper. 'Can you tell me anything else to narrow the search a little?'

Tom sat holding the drink of water Mr Lampard had given him. He carefully placed the glass on the table and coughed again.

'It's to do with…UFOs,' he said finally, fully expecting the old man to laugh and tell him *not to be so silly*, to *go and find something intelligent to read*, but instead he made an accepting noise in his throat and looked at Tom.

'Come on then, over here,' said Mr Lampard. Tom was taken by surprise and hurriedly followed his guide, turning the corner to find Mr Lampard scouring shelves with an extended finger, reading titles quietly to himself as he passed from spine to spine. 'Ah, here we are,' he said, tapping a book with a dark blue spine. He pulled it down and gave it to Tom.

Tom read the title: *UFO Sightings and Encounters*. He looked up and found Mr Lampard had another two books in his hand and was leading the way to a couple of chairs around a low table.

As he opened a book to its contents page, Mr Lampard was muttering *roz, roz* over and over again under his breath. 'That sounds familiar,' he said. 'I've heard that before.' His finger traced the chapters on the page and he stopped. 'Well, that looks promising.'

Under his finger it read, *The Roswell Conspiracy*. 'I think we might have something here – page 36.' He flicked the book open with practised fingers and sat up, his whole body language triumphant. He began to read.

'The Roswell Conspiracy is perhaps the world's most famous UFO story, capturing the imagination of millions and spawning numerous movies, books and television shows over the past fifty years.

The events of July 2nd 1947 are well documented. Around ten o'clock that evening an object was observed falling to earth outside Roswell, New Mexico, by Dan Wilmot. He described it as 'glowing,' and moving very quickly towards the north-west.

The next morning, local Rancher 'Mac' Brazel made an astonishing discovery. Thin foil-like wreckage lay scattered along a narrow stretch of land. On inspection, strange inscriptions which he likened to Egyptian hieroglyphics were found marking the surface of many pieces. He reported the material to be both unbendable and unbreakable.'

Tom listened in silence. When Mr Lampard finished reading he didn't know what to say. The importance of the few words he had heard the night before, as he fell towards sleep, now hit him hard – really hard.

'Does that sound about right? Is that what you're looking for?' Mr Lampard was looking at him with the book open in his palms.

Tom didn't know what to think so he nodded. His mind was racing. *Crashed UFOs. Wow!* Before he knew it he was asking a question aloud. 'What happened next?'

'Well, let's see.' Mr Lampard thumbed a few pages and clicked his tongue as he scanned the text. 'Well, it says here the military took the wreckage to Roswell Air Field. Included in the wreckage were *small grey figures, not unlike children in size,'* he quoted.

'Grey figures?' asked Tom, his mind now in even more of a whirl as something pitched around inside his head. He knew it was significant.

'Mm-hm.'

'So, where are they now?'

'Well, to find that out, I think you've got some reading to do, young man. If you believe it, of course,' added Mr Lampard with a smile.

Tom looked shocked. 'Why? Don't you?'

'Don't know if I do, don't know if I don't,' he replied sourly. 'I'm not one for superstitions and nonsense. Give me hard facts any day.'

'Aren't those hard facts?' asked Tom. 'The book says what happened.'

'Look at the title: *The Roswell Conspiracy*. Do you know what a conspiracy is?' He studied Tom closely.

'Well, no.'

Mr Lampard spoke slowly and clearly. 'A conspiracy is people working together on something secret, something not widely known about. It's often against the law as well. I think if you read this chapter carefully you'll find there's a reason why it's called The Roswell *Conspiracy*. I think you'll find it's not as clear as the book makes it.'

Tom sat back and thought for a moment, then stood up. 'May I take these books home, please?'

CHAPTER 24

A familiar song roused Mum from her doze. Yawning, she settled back in her seat, happy and relaxed as she whispered the lyrics to herself. The song soon faded and was replaced by the DJ's voice, jaunty and happy like Mum's mood. 'That was *I Love To Boogie* by Marc Bolan and T-Rex, a hit from 1976, but still sounding as good today.'

Mum smiled in agreement. She'd always been a fan even though she wasn't really old enough to remember much of the 1970s. Her brother Phillip had played T-Rex constantly as she was growing up, even more after Marc Bolan died in a car crash a year after the record had been a hit. Mum owed much of her love of 1970s music to her brother. *I must ring Phillip*, she thought. *I haven't spoken to him for ages.*

Abi stirred and let out a little sigh. The car was so quiet Mum had forgotten she was there. She opened her eyes and turned towards her sleeping daughter.

'Hey, sleepy head. You must have dozed off as well.' Abi opened her eyes and smiled. 'I guess that little walk tired us out more than we thought. It's only twenty-five past ten,' said Mum looking at her watch.

Abi opened her window, the heat now stifling. Mum's was already open, but, as the morning had grown warmer, the temperature inside the car had soared.

'I'm hungry,' said Abi, her stomach letting out a long, gurgling rumble. 'Can we get something to eat?'

'Come on, then,' said Mum. She started the car and pulled onto the main road. Roseberry Topping receded behind them as they turned off at the roundabout, following the signpost for Stokesley. Before long they were pulling into the high street with its cobbled parking spaces.

They passed a baker's shop and the promise of something sticky and tasty made Abi and Mum smile. 'Yummy, yummy,' said Abi, and they both laughed.

Mum pulled into a parking space and switched off the engine. Abi unclipped her seat belt and made to open her door, but, just as Mum was about to turn off the radio, a news jingle cut in and the announcer spoke, his voice clear now the engine had gone silent.

'This is the news at eleven thirty.'

Eleven thirty? Mum checked her watch. It only read ten thirty. *That's strange,* she thought. She picked up her mobile from the dashboard and looked at the display. Ten thirty.

'What's wrong?' Abi was half out of the car.

'My watch. The mobile. They both say it's ten thirty but the radio says it's eleven thirty. How can they both be wrong? They were right when we left this morning, so how can we be an hour behind? That doesn't make sense.'

The news reader's voice broke in on Mum's thoughts. He was half way through a report when Mum realised what he was saying.

'..were pursued by RAF fighters. Eyewitness reports claim the lights held formation over the Cleveland hills for several minutes before flying off at speed. The Ministry of Defence has declined to comment. In other news...'

Something seemed familiar about the story but Mum couldn't remember what. She shrugged and climbed out of the car, locking it behind her, before stepping onto the path. Taking Abi's hand, they chatted endlessly as they walked towards the bakery, their mood light. But in the back of Mum's mind something was nagging.

Why are the times exactly one hour slow?

* * *

Tom found an empty bench on the village green. He sat with the book Mr Lampard had been reading and read to the end of the chapter. Some of the words were really hard for him and he had to spend time breaking them down as he did in school, but he struggled on, regardless. It was slow going, but he was so engrossed in the book that he didn't want to stop.

He was surprised to read that the United States Government denied anything had happened at Roswell. At first they had allowed newspaper photographs to be published which showed some of the wreckage, along with the headline *RAAF Captures Flying Saucer on Ranch in Roswell Region.* There was even a photograph of Major Jesse Marcel with the wreckage, but the report was later said to be a mistake. A weather balloon had come down and that was all.

But as the years had passed, witnesses had come forward who said they had seen the bodies of the crew, but been told to keep quiet. Tom sat thinking. What was it Mr Lampard had said? *A conspiracy is something secret?*

Tom thought he was starting to understand.

* * *

Dad enjoyed the warmth of the summer wind, his elbow through the open window as the car sped along the country lanes. Mum and he had just dropped Danny off at Middlesbrough station where he had caught a train back to York on the promise that he would keep in touch. Both men had shaken hands with a new strength of feeling between them: they had rebuilt an important bond that should never have been broken and were determined not to let it slip again. Now, driving home, Dad felt good.

He chatted to Mum about the walk up to Eston Nab and how Danny and he had spent the day reminiscing about their childhood. They had enjoyed each other's company for the first time in nearly twenty years and had caught up on life's events. Spending a full day out together had been the perfect opportunity.

Both Mum and Dad were relaxed and happy. The day was beautiful and the countryside was where they were both very much at home. Dad had telephoned his boss that morning and arranged to take a few extra days off work. He now felt as though the whole family could spend some quality time together and do the things they had wanted to do for a while. He would be able to take Tom and Abi into the hills again as he had promised, and the thought made him feel good.

Mum suddenly remembered about her watch being wrong.

'You mean your watch was an hour slow?' Dad asked, feeling it was more likely that her watch had just stopped.

'Not just my watch, the time on my mobile was exactly an hour slow as well.' She pointed to the dashboard locker. 'I haven't changed the time yet because I wanted to show you. Don't you think it's strange?'

'It's probably just one of those things,' Dad replied. 'Your mobile's a few years' older than mine. It must be playing up. These things happen.' He picked the mobile out of the locker and looked at it.

Absently he looked at his own watch and had to do a double take as he realised it was showing exactly the same time.

16:22.

CHAPTER 25

Quietly, the evening drifted by. Mum and Dad sat in the garden with a bottle of wine, enjoying the pleasant warmth after the heat of the day, while Abi sat reading under the shade of the trees. Earlier, Tom had spent a few hours outside watching his Mum and Dad, but they had been too wrapped up in themselves to notice his attention on them.

He couldn't understand why they were so different. The early hours of this morning had been so frightening, so strange, and although they didn't seem to be bothered by any of it, to Tom it was still very real. He couldn't get it out of his head and after what he had read he was beginning to wonder if his life was ever going to be the same again.

Even Abi seemed different – lighter somehow. She had been so bubbly over tea, giggling over silly things that he'd thought he was in a different house.

Since Mum and Dad had picked him up from Mary's, nothing had seemed right. He had a definite feeling that something was amiss but couldn't put his finger on precisely what it was. Now, sat in the late evening warmth by his open bedroom window, he was engrossed in the books he had borrowed from the library. There was so much information in them that he started skipping through whole sections, finding much of it repeated in other books.

As he read, he became particularly interested in something known as "missing time", and the more he read, the more fascinated he became. It seemed to be a major part of the UFO phenomenon. He read numerous accounts of encounters and found that the same pattern of events was repeated again and again, but when his eyes begin to droop, and he could concentrate no more, he reluctantly closed the books and placed them beside his bed.

As the shadows began to lengthen towards nine o'clock Mum shouted up from the garden asking Tom to get ready for bed, but by then he was already asleep.

CHAPTER 26

Saturday morning was beautiful. Sunlight soaked the front of the Old Vicarage, slanting in through the windows of the kitchen and living room and turning it into an oven, even at such an early hour. A gentle breeze lifted the honeysuckle blossoms, causing them to flutter, their scent delicately sweet in the morning air. A cat lay stretched out in the warmth of the sun's rays, its paws turned upwards to soak up the early warmth, while a single white butterfly fluttered its way across the lawn, rising and falling like the crest of an invisible wave.

Rubbing the sleep from his eyes, Tom looked out of his bedroom window just in time to see the postman's head disappear from view beneath the window sill. A familiar *creak-click* followed and, after a few seconds, the figure returned, bending to fasten the latch on the garden gate, before briefly looking up. Tom returned his jaunty wave with a smile before stepping away from the window. Looking down he saw the books he had been reading the night before and bent to pick one up. As he flicked through it he remembered the startling accounts and whistled softly to himself. *Boy, oh boy*, he thought.

The page blurred and Tom rubbed his eyes, thinking some sleep still lingered there, but his mind flashed. He stumbled, dropping the book as he put out a hand to catch himself and leaned against the edge of the window, shaking his head to clear the fuzziness. He looked out at the sun drenched scenery and felt his heart slow, its beating seeming to take forever. A figure appeared before him, the same dark figure as the morning before, its face shrouded in shadow, its voice filling his thoughts and causing his head to swim. The sound was powerful and demanding inside his head.

You will soon understand. You must not let the knowledge die.

In the briefest of instants his world seemed to stretch in all directions, stars and planets expanding, his consciousness plunged deep within them. He had a sense of eternity and a flash of ending, of finality, of drawing to a close. An overwhelming sense of doom accompanied the visions, and instantly Tom understood that his involvement, his very place within it, was not by chance.

The thoughts dissipated and left his mind empty before another sensation took its place. The sensation of familiarity touched his mind like the tender caress of a hand, and with it a layer of kindness and helpfulness interwoven with a coldness of intelligence.

As the voice flooded his mind a final time, its words echoing inside his head, he knew instantly where he had sensed it before.

When the time is right, you must speak for our species.

And then it was gone, as if it had never been there at all.

* * *

Dad was nearly at the top of the stairs when the letterbox creaked. A few letters clattered to the stone floor while something larger was thrust into the opening. After a brief struggle, it dropped to the mat and the letterbox clicked shut, the sound loud as it echoed up the hallway. Dad leaned over the banister in an attempt to see what had been delivered but couldn't make out more than the edges of a few envelopes. *Looks like bills* he thought to himself and continued on towards the bathroom, muttering to himself as he went. *More money!*

Slippers scuffed their way towards the front door and Mum bent to pick up the untidy pile. She shuffled the envelopes and brightly coloured leaflets advertising *Food At The Lowest Prices Around* and the opportunity to *Be A Winner – No Purchase Necessary* into one hand as she held the small yellow parcel in the other, turning it over to read the address label. She instantly recognised the handwriting printed across the front in bold capitals: it was Dad's. *That's strange, she thought.* Turning it over once more she gave it a quick shake before placing it beside the telephone and proceeded to separate the bills from the junk mail. An envelope addressed to *Mrs. D Richards* in a neat handwritten script attracted her attention and she placed the bills on top of the small parcel, thumbing open the top of the envelope. Pulling the enclosed letter free, she unfolded it and smiled as she realised it was from her friend Kitty in Manchester. She turned and walked slowly back towards the kitchen without looking up.

Covered by brown envelopes, the small yellow parcel lay hidden. When Dad at last came downstairs he glanced at the envelopes, without moving them, and made a small sound of disgust under his breath. Then he stepped towards the kitchen, intent on his first coffee of the morning.

Tom sat eating a bowl of cereal, his thoughts somewhere between the events of the night before last and the contents of the books he had read. His mind was in a

119

whirl and he needed to sort it out. He didn't want to talk to Mum and Dad about it; in fact he didn't want to talk to anyone at all. He couldn't, not until he understood what it was all about. He had some serious thinking and hopefully some understanding to do today.

Having finished his cereal, Tom dropped the bowl into the sink and watched it float for a few seconds. It swung from side to side as narrow dribbles of water trickled over the edge and puddled in the bottom, mixing with the dregs of the milk. When it filled with soapy water and sank from sight, he stood looking around the kitchen.

'You alright, sport?'

Tom smiled as his Dad entered. 'Yeah. Fine, thanks.' He didn't feel fine but wasn't up to explaining.

'Gonna be another nice day. Fancy a walk later? We could go up to The Monument if you like.' Dad always called Captain Cook's Monument up on Easby Moor, *The Monument*.

Tom thought for a second, his mind running over the content of the books. Images of black triangles and lights whirled around his brain with the speed of an express train, and he shivered. Dad didn't seem to notice.

Finally he found his voice. 'Yeah, but maybe later? After lunch?'

'Fine.' Dad smiled his *catch you later* smile and turned back towards the living room where he picked up the morning paper and plonked himself in the chair by the window.

Tom stood and watched his Dad. He couldn't believe what he was seeing; neither Mum, Dad nor Abi seemed even slightly bothered about the other night. None of them had mentioned it yesterday after returning from their day out, yet only hours before they had been so stunned by what they had experienced that they had barely been able to speak.

That's not right, he thought. What's going on? What in the world is going on?

* * *

Mum and Dad were laughing at a shared joke when Tom stepped through the kitchen door an hour later. Abi was pouring herself a drink of orange and Tom was instantly thirsty at the sight of it.

'Pass me a glass, please,' he asked and Abi opened the cupboard. She handed him a tall glass without a word and he half filled it from the jug. Abi didn't smile and Tom looked at her closely. He didn't like what he saw. 'You're very quiet today. You alright?'

She smiled. 'Just don't feel like talking much.' Picking up her glass she walked into the hallway, the breeze from the open back door fluttering her hair gently. It shone like gold, almost white in the brightness of the sun and an image of bright lights suddenly flashed through Tom's mind. He felt himself jolt, his glass shattering as it hit the stone floor, fragments scattering in all directions while juice flowed in narrow rivers between the cracks of the stone flags.

'What...?' Mum started towards Tom but Dad was closer. He squatted down and began picking up pieces of glass. 'Don't move and don't touch anything.' Mum laid a tea towel on the floor and together they began picking up the pieces.

She looked up from the floor by Tom's feet. 'What happened?'

'I…I don't know,' he mumbled. 'I think it just slipped.'

'Don't move until we've cleared it all up.' Dad's voice was sterner than he intended but then he stopped, his hand mid way between the floor and the open tea towel. In his hand he held a triangular shard of glass. He was staring at it.

'What's wrong?'

Dad didn't speak. He remained crouched where he was, the shard of glass gripped between finger and thumb. He looked at Mum but she couldn't read his expression. 'This reminds me of something, but I don't know what.' His voice was quiet. 'Something I should know about.' He stared at Mum and she raised her eyebrows, shaking her head slowly.

Dad remained crouched for a few seconds then slowly, deliberately, placed the glass in the tea towel with the other pieces. 'It's gone,' he said finally. 'Whatever it was, it's gone now.'

Mum picked up the tea towel and carefully placed it on the table. 'Now, you be more careful,' she said reprovingly to Tom as she opened the cupboard. Tom looked shocked; the image of lights was still fresh in his mind and Mum touched his cheek gently, mistaking his expression for something else. When she spoke her voice was softer than before. 'It's alright, honest.' Tom looked up and saw a warm smile but his own wasn't so convincing.

Behind her, Abi walked into the kitchen and placed her empty glass on the table. She held something out to Dad. 'What's this?' she asked. In her hand she held a yellow packet.

CHAPTER 27

Dad took the parcel and turned it over curiously.

'Oh, that came in the post for you this morning. I meant to tell you but I think you were in the bathroom. Sorry.' Mum made an apologetic face as she dried her hands. 'It looks like your handwriting,' she added. 'Have you ordered something?'

'Don't think so.' Dad started picking at the seal and was soon rummaging around inside the envelope. With two fingers he pulled out a small rectangular box and held it up.

'A tape?' asked Mum. 'Does it say anything on it?'

Dad opened the case and tipped the microcassette out into the palm of his hand. He dropped the envelope onto the table and another tape clattered out onto the dark wood. He picked it up. 'This one says *Tape 2*. Why would I be sending myself micro cassettes?' then corrected himself. 'I haven't sent myself anything.'

'When you were in the car yesterday this was in your pocket,' said Tom, picking up the envelope. 'You kept fiddling with it, checking it was still there.'

'Yesterday?' Dad was confused.

'You must have gone to the Post Office in Great Ayton when Mum took me to Mary's. You and Danny went somewhere, don't you remember?'

'We went to buy a paper but didn't go anywhere near the Post Office.' Dad took the envelope from Tom and turned it over, inspecting it. 'I don't remember this.'

Abi spoke softly from the other end of the table. 'Why don't you listen to it?' She stood by the open drawer, a black Dictaphone held out before her. For a few seconds Dad didn't move, then he reached out and took it from her. Inserting *Tape 1* he sat down and pressed the play button.

The tape hissed and banged for a short time before settling, and then a voice boomed from the tiny loudspeaker.

It was Danny's.

CHAPTER 28

Danny's voice sounded nervous.

'This whole thing…it's…it's like nothing you've ever thought about or heard before.'

Sound betrayed someone's movements: a clinking of glass and the turning on of a tap. After a brief pause the voice continued.

'It's going to blow the lid off so many ideas, so many theories and religious beliefs. Beliefs about the world and where we came from. It's going to blow them wide open, Pete. It's going to blow them wide open and it's going to change everything. Absolutely everything.'

'What do you mean? You've got to tell me. I've got to make some sense of what happened tonight.'

Dad picked up the tape machine and pressed stop. 'I haven't had this conversation. We sat here talking the other night, we all did, remember? But this conversation,' he held up the Dictaphone, 'this never happened.'

'It must have. That's Danny's voice, unless it's from a long time ago.'

'These things weren't around when we were kids,' said Dad gesturing with the Dictaphone again. 'We couldn't have afforded one even if they were.'

Abi was looking inside the envelope. 'There's something else in here.' She fished out a folded piece of paper and gave it to Dad. When he opened it he raised his eyebrows at the content and then, with a deep breath, read the top line. 'It's dated 12th August. That's yesterday.'

'What does it say?' Mum was intrigued.

Dad took another breath and continued.

'Pete,

When you receive this parcel the chances are you won't remember anything about it. You won't recall having the conversation you are about to hear, and when you have listened to it you won't believe it.

But it's all true. It really is.

Before you listen you need to be prepared to rethink your understanding of so many things you have come to believe in, things you have come to trust in. What you are going to hear will be hard to understand, hard to believe, but it is real.

Please believe it.'

Dad looked up. 'It's signed by Danny.' He passed it slowly over to Mum. 'And it's signed by me.'

Mum read it through to herself and laughed. 'This is your idea of a joke. Both of you. You're making up for lost time, aren't you? You decided to play one last joke on us before Danny went home. I know you did. It's a prank.' She pushed her chair back and stood up, the letter fluttering onto the table. 'Gotcha!' She pointed directly at Dad and grinned.

Dad didn't laugh. He didn't stand up and say, *okay, you got me. Yeah, we thought we'd pull one on you. Took us all night but it was a good 'un.* Instead he sat there and looked at Mum. 'Debs, it's no joke. I promise.' His voice was very

126

quiet, his face serious.

Mum's smile faltered. 'Are you sure?'

Dad nodded.

Slowly she pulled the chair underneath herself and sat down again. 'Pete, if this is some kind of a joke, I'm gonna kill you!'

Dad shook his head. 'No joke. I promise.' He took a long breath, let it out slowly, and pressed play.

'The human race has been here for what? Two million years? Well, we need to go back beyond that, back to the start of everything: time, the universe, and even further back than that.'

'What? There isn't anything before that. There's nothing before the start of the universe, before the Big Bang. There is no "before".'

Dad sounded puzzled.

'You need to stop thinking that way. I want you to open your mind to the idea that anything and everything you've ever heard could be wrong. Or, at least, not as you've understood it, because everything the human race thinks it understands about physics and the creation of the universe is about to be turned on its head.'

Danny paused before continuing, as if collecting his thoughts.

'When we were younger I believed in the possibility of life elsewhere, on other planets, remember?'

'Mmhmm.'

'Well, after a while I started seeing things. Nothing I couldn't explain, though. But when I was focused on things – I

127

mean really focused, like being totally engrossed in a book or working out something that needed all my concentration – I'd become aware that something was…well, watching me. It was as if they were studying me, observing everything I did.'

'I began to think it was just my imagination, but then I'd see faces at the fringe of my vision although they were never quite in focus. It was as if they were hiding in my mind's-eye, but when I tried to look they were gone. I never caught them and started to believe that it was my imagination running away with me – that my sub-conscious mind was playing tricks and I became used to almost seeing these 'Watchers' on a regular basis. They didn't frighten me because they were familiar. It was almost comforting to know that they were there, the way the marks on the back of your hand are always there. They're a part of what makes you…well, you.'

Dad mumbled a reply but the tape barely picked it up.

'Or the way your watch becomes like an extension of your body. If you forget to put it on you can almost feel it there on your wrist, even though it's not there at all. I bet that sounds daft, but that's the way it was.'

'And then purely by chance I found out that someone way back in my family had been a medium, able to talk to the spirits. I'd never heard about them before but I began to wonder if somehow I was experiencing the same kind of thing. So I looked into it. Of course there was no way to test it and it just stayed as a thought, a possibility. I stored it away in the back of my mind and that was it.'

'Around the time that we were thirteen or fourteen I began to hear whispers. They seemed to be there when I was totally engrossed in whatever I was doing. Sometimes they were there

with the Watchers, sometimes not. I could never understand what they were saying. It was like listening to voices in another room with the door shut, or the radio late at night when the reception is poor and the stations are crossed. You know that something is being said but you can't hear quite what. If I tried to listen a bit too hard they would stop, as if they were aware of me listening and didn't want me to hear what they were saying.'

'But, when I was fifteen, it all stopped. They just went away and my head seemed empty. I was so used to them being there that when they disappeared it was as if some part of me was missing, as if it had been removed.'

Danny paused. When he continued his voice was trembling.

'But that was the easy bit to deal with, because, when they came back, they came for more.'

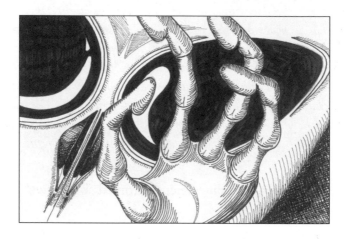

CHAPTER 29

'*What do you mean, more?*'

Dad's voice was curious. He also sounded nervous.

'*They came back and they took me.*'

It was possible to hear Danny shudder, even over the tape.

'*When you say they 'took' you, do you mean they actually...'took' you?*'

'*Yes.*'

The tape went quiet for a while; the only sound was of someone moving.

'*What do you remember?*'

When Danny spoke again his voice was quiet,

thoughtful, and full of fear.

'*A bright, very intense light shone from somewhere above. I was in bed but somehow it penetrated the ceiling. For some reason I wasn't at all frightened, in fact, there was a feeling of total calm and I remember wondering where the light was coming from.*'

'*What happened next?*'

'*A sensation of floating and a feeling of cold was followed by enveloping warmth. I was aware it was a cold night outside but that didn't seem to matter. I had a feeling of sudden movement, like you feel when a lift starts to drop, except it was upwards and was much faster.*'

'*You were abducted? Don't people who are abducted have to undergo hypnosis to remember what happened to them?*'

'*Usually. Before the other day I wouldn't have remembered any of this.*'

Danny took a long shuddering breath.

'*This is the hard bit. You remember I talked about the faces in my mind's eye? Well, they weren't in my mind's eye any longer. They were there, above me – long pointed faces with penetrating black eyes.*'

The voice began to tremble, tears hiding behind it but ready to push forward at any moment.

'*Those eyes and those long, almost skeletal hands with pointed fingertips. They scratched and scraped over my skin, probing me with needle-like instruments; eyes, ears, stomach, genitals. They took bits of me and didn't care that it hurt. God, did it hurt!*'

Danny was sobbing, his breath racked and gasping with the memory. Dad spoke soothingly, trying to calm his friend. Eventually the tape ran out and the Dictaphone clicked off.

Nobody spoke. What could they possibly say? Their thoughts swam with the enormity of the revelations they had just heard, until finally Dad picked up the Dictaphone and turned the tape over. The silence between them was almost too much to bear.

Danny's voice sounded calmer now, as if he at last had some control over his emotions. He continued.

'They took me three times in the months between my sixteenth and seventeenth birthdays. It was the same each time: the light, the sensation of floating, the sudden movement and the examinations. But then it all stopped, suddenly and without warning.'

He blew out a breath, the relief in his voice evident for all to hear.

'They didn't come for me again.'

The sound of a drink being poured filled the tape for long seconds. Danny made a few false starts, trying to find the words he so badly needed to verbalise what he had to say. Somehow Dad knew that whatever came next was going to be big.

'They didn't come for me again until this week, but this time it was different. This time they called me and I went to them.'

'They called you?'

'The only way I can describe it is…it was like being pulled

along in a dream from which you cannot wake. You know you're walking about, doing all the things you normally do but it's as if you are still asleep. I suppose it was some kind of waking dream.'

'What do you remember?'

'Walking, an intense thirst and a sensation of burning. I remember walking across the hilltops and I could see Eston Nab in the distance. I was aware that I was somewhere near the old ironstone mines.'

'And then there was the light again, except this time it came from inside the hills, as if the rock had opened up and swallowed me.'

'The tunnels opened into a larger chamber supported by pillars. The roof was supported in many places but these had given way over time and much of the roof had come down.'

Danny paused to clear his throat before continuing.

'Time passed – I really don't know how long – but I became aware of small lights darting around me.'

Tom sat back and pursed his lips. He remembered the night before last and understood the relevance of Danny's words, but Mum and Dad just stared at each other vacantly. They didn't know what to make of it.

'The tunnel seemed to enlarge and distort before me, the ceiling lifting and expanding as the wooden beams bent and twisted, forming a spherical chamber where I rested.'

'I was aware of whispering voices inside my head – the familiar voices of my youth – but this time they were more intense. This time they seemed to be in conflict. Then suddenly they stopped and everything was silent. Their presence deserted me for a time and I could have slept. I honestly don't know.'

The tape hissed for nearly a minute. Dad picked up the Dictaphone and checked to see if the tape was still running, but as he held it Danny started speaking again.

'*I became aware of…some kind of presence inside my mind, movement not unlike an electrified tingle running through my muscles and I could feel it looking at me – no, not looking at me, looking into me.*'

'*When the voices came back they were erratic and there was an overwhelming sense of anxiety. Something was definitely wrong and the only way I can describe it is panic. My head suddenly felt crammed and I couldn't cope with the pressure. It was as if my head were going to explode.*'

'*And then the visions came. They were unlike anything I could have ever imagined; awesome in their scale as they swam into and over each other but I couldn't focus clearly. It was as if my head was being twisted inside out.*'

Danny began to cry. He sobbed uncontrollably and the tape clicked as it was paused. When his voice returned it was whispered, barely in control.

'*What I saw was a mistake. Somehow I was exposed to visions and knowledge that were not mine to see. Some people might say the visions I've seen are a privilege, an opportunity to reach out and touch the universe, but I wouldn't. After what they did to me, after what I've seen, I wouldn't wish them on anyone. I'd call them a curse.*'

CHAPTER 30

The tape switched itself off and a heavy silence hung in the air. Abi disappeared into the living room and curled up on the sofa. Mum followed. They chatted for a few minutes and when Mum returned to the kitchen she closed the door quietly behind her. Abi didn't want to hear anymore.

Mum stood shuffling the junk mail into a pile on the unit top, more for something to do than any other reason, and then turned to face Dad. 'Do you want to hear the rest?'

Dad was pale. He looked at Mum, his eyes like those of a frightened animal. 'I've got to.'

'Well I don't, and I don't think Tom should either.' She turned towards Tom. 'You go on up to your room. This isn't suitable for you.'

Tom nearly exploded. 'Am I the only one who remembers what happened the other night?'

'The other night?'

'The black ship!'

'What are you talking about?' Dad folded his arms and frowned.

'The night before last. Don't you remember? The ship? The lights? The vibration?' He looked directly at his Mum. 'Don't you remember? The figures outside? On the lawn?' He stared in disbelief as his parents shook their heads. 'The Greys!' He almost shouted it across the table.

Tom sat wide eyed with disbelief. 'What about your

watches and the mobile being an hour slow? Don't you think that's strange?'

'Well….' Mum seemed unsure. She exchanged glances with Dad but he didn't speak.

Tom changed his approach, speaking directly to Dad.

'When you and Danny were talking the other night I heard you mention Roswell.' He turned to his Mum. 'I looked it up yesterday. When you took me to Mary's, she let me go to the library. I've even got the books upstairs. Mum, there was a UFO crash at Roswell in 1947.'

'That doesn't – '

Tom cut his Dad off. 'And Rendlesham Forest? Something happened there as well.' He paused, unsure what to say next. 'Those things outside the other night, the bright lights, both your watches being an hour slow, they're all to do with UFOs. They're all things that happen!' Tom let his words sink in for a moment. 'Don't you remember running out onto the lawn as the ship took off? And the fighters? You must remember the fighters that flew over and chased it? Don't you remember anything? Anything at all?'

'Well…I…' Dad didn't have a chance to finish. Mum changed the tape and pressed the 'Play' button.

CHAPTER 31

'I don't know how I found my way back onto the hillside or to here. All I know is I woke up in your home with the sensation of being watched, but it makes some kind of sense now. I realise that everything – the visions, the voices, everything that's inside my head – shouldn't be there at all. I know who they are and I know why they're here.'

'So who are they?'

'I always called them the Watchers, but they have another name. They call themselves the An'Tsari. The Seeders.'

'Seeders?'

'Yes, because that's what they do.'

Danny paused, took a deep breath and held it for a few seconds before letting it out noisily.

'The An'Tsari, the Seeders, are very old. They are older than any concept of time we have and yet they've always been here, even before time as we understand it began.'

'That's impossible.'

Danny ignored the interruption.

They came from somewhere outside of our knowledge and understanding, and have been watching us forever.'

'Forever? Why, what's so important about us?'

'It's not who we are, it's what we are. It's the thing that makes us…us. Our genetic make-up. Our genes. Our DNA.'

Dad made as if to speak but only succeeded in uttering a confused sound. He didn't know what to say.

'You see our DNA is complex, it's highly specific. It makes us who we are, but make any changes to our DNA and, well…we change. That's basic biology.'

'I understand that, but why are they so interested in ours?'

'Because our DNA is unique. So unique, in fact, that they're taking samples and guarding it.'

'Guarding it?'

'You see the whole universe is constantly changing, and with it billions of DNA strands are growing and evolving at any one time.'

Dad's voice was excited.

'You mean there's other life in the universe, apart from us and these…these Greys?'

'*Yes.*'

A pause.

Danny jumped ahead.

'*They've been visiting us for a long time, watching us and collecting our DNA. They've tried to keep themselves hidden from us and in most cases they've managed it, but occasionally something which they can't control, something they can't predict, exposes them.*'

'*You mean like Roswell?*'

'*Exactly. The Roswell crash was an accident. It wasn't supposed to happen. They had been retrieving data from one of the many probes they have here – they're spread out over the entire face of the globe but always well-hidden, burrowed into mountain sides, under the sands of the Sahara desert, in the deepest parts of the ocean – but occasionally, during retrieval, the Seeders are seen.*'

'*At Roswell something happened and their ship clipped the hillside. It ploughed into the desert and scattered debris over a wide area. And the rest, as they say, is history.*'

'*And what about Rendlesham Forest?*'

'*Everyone takes a chance sometimes, right?*'

Dad mumbled his agreement.

'*Well sometimes it pays off and sometimes it doesn't. Rendlesham Forest was one of those occasions where it didn't go their way. They tried to retrieve data from a probe that was about to fail. If it had shut down they would have lost everything. Unfortunately they were seen, but they tried again* the following night. The same happened. The probe eventually failed.'

'What about other sightings around the world?'

'Most of them are purely unfortunate. You see, as people have become more aware of the UFO phenomenon they are more attuned to watching for them. It's like a downward spiral: the more they are seen, the more people look for them.'

'The worst situation was over Belgium in 1990. They have a ship which spends its time jumping between universes, retrieving data from automated Seeker probes and Workerships – what we call UFOs – so it can be processed and stored until needed. The ship was overdue and when it arrived, the decision was made to approach earth closer than ever before to speed up the rate of transfer. It was while the Workerships were all clustered to the underside that they were seen. Triangular formations of white lights were seen by thousands of people as they orbited the earth. On that day the An'Tsari made a bad decision.'

'So they are collecting our DNA and storing it. Why? I thought you said life was everywhere in the universe.'

Danny's voice dropped almost to a whisper.

'It is, but not in the way you think.'

CHAPTER 32

'This is like science fiction,' said Dad, stunned. 'It's unbelievable!'

Mum sat, her face a blank mask. She gestured to Dad to start the tape again. She was as interested as everyone else to see where this was going.

'Think of it like this: the universe is a tapestry, its threads of evolution intertwined with billions of others across space and time. But as some unravel others hold on, their ability to do that dictated by the strength of their thread. Now think of those threads as a universe full of life. If they were to unravel totally, then the life they represent would die.'

'I still don't understand the connection with us.'

'We are the single thread which holds the universe together.'

'Us?'

'Human DNA is unique. It is the foundation of the universe.'

'Hang on, hang on, let me think this through for a minute. You're telling me that our DNA is everywhere?'

'Yes.'

'The foundation?'

'Yes.'

'But you said these Watchers, these Seeders, whatever you

want to call them, are older than us, have been around since before time began.'

'They have.'

'Well, how can that be? If our DNA is everywhere – you said yourself we are the foundation of the universe, and yet they are older than us – then their DNA must predate ours.' Dad paused. *'I'm lost. I don't understand.'*

'You will. What do you know about the Big Bang?'

'The Big Bang? It created the universe. It was the explosion which started everything.'

'Right. And what do you know about the Big Crunch?'

'The Big Crunch? That's the opposite. When the universe stops expanding it will start to contract again until one day, billions of years from now, it will collapse in on itself and that will be the end of it. The Big Crunch. The end.'

Danny spoke very softly.

'No, it won't.'

'What do you mean?'

Movement. The sound of a magazine being opened and a page being torn out.

'Think of the universe as existing on one side of this sheet of paper. Now what if I told you another universe, probably with another you and me, existed on the other side? They're right next to each other but we can't see them and they can't see us. Neither of us knows the other is there. A parallel universe.'

'I've heard these theories. Albert Einstein. Stephen Hawking. They both reckon there are multiple universes layered one on top of another.'

'You've got it. Now imagine all the pages of this magazine are universes. Watch what happens when I close it. The sheets are now on top of one another: multiple, parallel universes all existing alongside each other within the same space.'

Dad whistled.

'And if I cut a hole through the middle I can, in theory, pass from one universe to another. All I have to do is travel through the hole.'

'And that's...?'

'Yes, that's what they're doing; they're moving from one universe to another. They're opening doorways of some kind – don't ask me how, of that I have no idea – and they are moving through them from one universe to another.'

'This might sound like a totally dumb question, but why?'

'Well that's the reason behind everything. As each universe is created they seed it with DNA, then they watch for the first signs of life to evolve. They seek out the strongest strains, harvest it, catalogue it and store it. They've been doing this since before time as we understand it began, even before our universe was created.'

'Before our Big Bang they were in another universe. A parallel universe. When they left they took with them all they had collected and came here. Our universe was fresh and young. It was in its infancy and to ensure the existence of life they seeded our universe with human DNA from other universes. That *way, human evolution was assured.'*

'But why seed it from other universes? If there's already life here...?'

'Don't you see? That's the whole point. There isn't any. In its purest, most basic form the universe is barren and lifeless. Without seeding, life won't evolve anywhere, in this universe or in any other.'

'But if human DNA didn't evolve unaided – you said yourself it needed seeding – then, where did it come from? Where did it first evolve?'

Silence. When Dad spoke again his voice was tight with shock.

'Oh, God. You mean...?'

'Yes. Them.'

CHAPTER 33

Sleep came with its share of dreams.

Tom tossed and turned for hours as he mulled over everything he had heard, trying to comprehend the magnitude of what he now knew. Eventually, after much relentless pondering he had drifted off, but his sleep was not tranquil.

Danny's voice had echoed through his dreams, his recorded words swirling round in a jumble that made no sense. Tom woke on several occasions and heard the voices of Mum and Dad talking quietly downstairs. When he looked at the clock it showed the time was just after one, then two thirty, but finally he settled into sleep. The tensions of the past twenty four hours left his confused brain, and his rest was at last so deep that his mind began to relax.

His subconscious was awoken by a presence. It wormed

its way into his mind, finding a place to conceal itself while studying his memories.

It didn't take long to find what Tom had learned and set about accessing his dream-state, working its way in so he would absorb the knowledge the presence brought with it. A warm and familiar voice reached out.

Tom responded.

Who are you?

You know who I am, but that is not important.

Tom sensed friendliness, inquisitiveness and strength.

Mr Lampard?

The question was not answered, but Tom felt a familiarity entwined with something unknown.

The presence continued.

My time is limited. It is urgent that I leave you with that which you will need.

What I will need?

A feeling of urgency.

Are you ready?

No. I don't understand. Who are you?

That will become clear.

Urgency.

The human species is evolving, as is your place within the universe.

Our place?

Your place and your responsibility. They cannot be ignored.

Why are you telling me this? I…

You have a knowledge nobody else possesses. You will know when to use it and your planet will listen.

What knowledge?

Simply this: the protection we offered is no longer required.

What do you mean?

We are unable to protect and re-seed the human species beyond the present.

Why?

An overwhelming sense of conclusion.

Finality.

Is the human race dying?

No, you are evolving. We are dying.

Why?

All things must die, that is the way of the universe. The race of time is something even we cannot win.

But if you die who will seed the universe?

A pause.

Do you not understand the consequences of your evolution? Your species is unique. You will know what to do.

How? We are not like you.

You will evolve, you will adapt and you will learn. You have the potential, the resilience and the strength to find that which you will need. Your origins, our origins, must not be forgotten.

Why are you telling me this?

The Elders believe our passing should be dignified by silence, that all we have become should draw to a close as this universe dies and life should find its own way, or fade. They believe we have done enough. Yet there are those within us who do not believe fate is an acceptable alternative. We wish to ensure life has the opportunity to survive and we believe our knowledge should not be lost.

Within us there is a growing desire for everything we have been to live on through another.

Who?

The knowledge you will possess will ensure our time in the universe – the accumulation of our knowledge, our experiences and our existence – will not end as the stars must end. The universe must know its origins. It must know from where it came. And it must continue.

What can I do? I am only a child. Nobody will believe me.

When the time is right they will. You will understand.

Understand what?

A pause, as if something waiting to be said was being held back.

Finally.

You will find it.

Find what?

Silence.

Mr Lampard?

Silence.

CHAPTER 34

Tom rolled over and opened his eyes. Instantly he felt a dull ache lodged at the base of his skull. He tried to ignore the pain but found it would not go away, his head thudding as though he had fallen and bumped it. Closing his eyes again, his head was instantly filled with images of drifting sand which swirled and cascaded in familiar patterns, yet any understanding of the visions seemed to lay just beyond his reach. And through it all, an impression of something important tantalised his dreams.

When he awoke half an hour later his headache was almost gone. Climbing slowly from his bed, he drew back the curtains and stood gazing across the sunlit fields, his mind racing as he struggled to make sense of his dreams.

An overwhelming sense of being drawn towards something he did not understand suddenly overtook him, and from that moment on Tom Richards knew his life was going to be different.

CHAPTER 35

Eternal darkness. Eternal night. Shattered forever by cataclysmic explosions of matter and energy, boiling and churning through the countless millennia, rushing and expanding until, finally, after a universal wink of an eye, they slowed and they cooled.

Gases coalesced, countless suns were born and barren worlds evolved, lived and died.

First Creation.

In their youth they were inquisitive, impetuous even, the universe their playground. But as the eons passed and they matured they saw the desolate nature of everything with new eyes. And they longed for contact with another.

Moving from Universe to Universe they found the pattern repeated; a barren, desolate wasteland, and their conscience could not allow this to continue. Through each planetary cycle of birth, life and death they watched, they learnt and they grew, and finally their place in the universe was ordained.

The spark of life which had lifted them from the seas of their long-dead home world must be rekindled – reborn. It must not be allowed to die.

And so, on a planet still cooling from the effects of its fiery birth, they seeded.

GLOSSARY

Chapter 2:   **fresh orange** - freshly squeezed orange juice, also known as juice

Chapter 2:   **tutting** - a sound made with the tongue to show disapproval

Chapter 2:   **keeping her tongue between her teeth** – an attempt to not say something; to bite your tongue

Chapter 2:   **mucky article** - an affectionate northern expression used to describe someone who is dirty, muddy or filthy

Chapter 3:   **treacle** – a sweet tasting syrup made from sugar; also known as molasses

Chapter 3:   **Bluebottle** - a large fly with a metallic blue abdomen

Chapter 5:   **screwed up his eyes** – to squint against a bright light

Chapter 7:   **heather** – a coarse purple shrub found growing over much of the Cleveland Hills

Chapter 7:   **bracken** – a fern; the most commonly found plant in the English countryside

Chapter 8:   **spindles** – the decorative wooden rails of a staircase which support the banister rail

Chapter 9:   **eddies** – circular movements of air

Chapter 11: **trainers** – training shoes; running shoes; pumps

Chapter 13: **trawled** – to trawl; to scour; to search carefully for something

Chapter 18: **chirping and trilling** – noises made by singing birds

Chapter 20: **pub** – a public house or bar

Chapter 20: **kerb** – kerb stone; the stone edging to a pavement or sidewalk

Chapter 21: **biscuit tin** – cookie jar

Chapter 24: **rucksack** – a bag worn on the back; a backpack or knapsack

Chapter 22: **thrush** – a song-bird known for its beautiful song; also known as a song thrush

Chapter 22: **goose-bumps** – goose-flesh; goose-pimples; small pimples on the skin in response to cold